THE PHANTOM AUTOMOBILES

A

GORDON

GARDNER

MYSTERY

SCOTT DENNIS PARKER

QUADRANT FICTION STUDIO

2015

The Phantom Automobiles

A Gordon Gardner Mystery

Copyright © 2015 by Scott Dennis Parker

A Quadrant Fiction Studio Book

(QFS-002)

www.QuadrantFictionStudio.com

This is a work of fiction. The characters, incidents, and dialogues are products of the author's imagination and are not to be construed as real.

ISBN-13: 978-0692461174
ISBN-10: 0692461175

Cover design by Scott Dennis Parker
Cover images:
Top: zimmytws
Bottom: tcharts

www.ScottDennisParker.com

Give feedback on the book at:

scott@scottdennisparker.com

Twitter: @sdparker7

Second Edition

Printed in the U.S.A

SHINING THE LIGHT OF JUSTICE!

Lucy Barnes gave Gordon a questioning look. "What's the scoop on that other thing you were so passionate about?"

"The Tompkins story? It was printed in the crime beat this morning. Officially, it's done."

"You satisfied with that?"

"Nope."

"You going to do anything about it?"

"I'm thinking about it."

"C'mon, buy me a cup of coffee and tell me what we're going to do next."

He led her to his car and they drove to a nearby Shipley Do-Nut shop. Over coffee and doughnuts, he related what he had learned about Tompkins—not much—his suspicions about Kernow—not much—and his ideas on how they were related.

"So you don't have much?" Lucy said.

"Nothing more than a hunch."

"How far do your hunches usually go?"

"To the front page."

She pursed her lips. "What do you want? The front page or the truth?"

He sat a moment thinking.

"Let me put it another way: are you still thinking about it because you want the story or are you wanting to uncover some secret?"

Gordon arranged the napkin and coffee cup in a precise order and used his finger to collect the crumbs. "With Victor Tompkins dead, Naomi and her husband now have to figure out what to do with their elderly mother. That was Victor's job. Now, whether it was merely an accident or an accident that could have been prevented, I aim to find out. Victor Tompkins clearly experienced something that made him think the cars were phantoms and I think it has something to do with the medicine he was taking. Why else would an otherwise normal man start thinking that kind of thing? So, that's what I'm gonna do. And I don't care if it gets me in hot water with Levitz. It's the right thing to do."

Lucy Barnes stood. "That's my kind of righteousness. What's our next move, Ace?"

To Vanessa who is always there
to keep me grounded

CHAPTER ONE

"I've got two dead bodies." Elijah Levitz, the editor of the *Houston Post-Dispatch*, flipped two pieces of paper between the fingers of each hand. "I'm gonna let one of my two junior ace reporters pick first."

Gordon Gardner inwardly bristled at the word 'junior' but knew he'd one day be the senior ace reporter. He stood in the main newsroom with the other reporters and hoped he got first pick. Having successfully flirted with the editor's secretary long enough to get the gists of both stories, Gordon knew which one of the stories would have the privilege of bearing his personal "Gordon Gardner" stamp.

But which one would he get?

When Levitz had called the meeting, the news hounds gathered liked sheep to a shepherd around Levitz. The portly man constantly had his necktie loosened. His open collar dirty around the inside ring, and a cigarette hung from dry lips. The unlit stick bobbed up and down as he spoke and handed out assignments. Each assignment was on a slip of paper torn from a stack held together by an iron rod and a cast-iron nut. Levitz claimed it was a piece of the Hindenburg. Few believed him although no reporter, copy boy, or secretary ever said so to his face.

When Levitz called out a story and assigned a reporter, that man would plow through the throng and snatch a piece of paper Levitz handed out.

Barbara Essary, the editor's secretary, sat at a nearby

desk and jotted notes. Sometimes they swapped stories. As a rule, Levitz didn't mind except in those times when he reminded his reporters that he was the editor and he assigned the stories as he saw fit.

This was one of those times.

"I think we all know which ones I'm talking about," Levitz continued. "There's the crazy guy who jumped in front of a moving car and lost, and the mugging death of William Silber, local artist. The latter's more of a fancy obit, the former's just a basic crime-blotter filler piece."

Gordon looked down and reread the slip of paper listing the job already assigned: a puff piece on the local nightclub owner, Bruno Clavell. Bruno had recently built his first club in Houston after a successful string of similar nightclubs in Dallas, Ft. Worth, San Antonio, and Austin. It didn't amount to much, but Gordon would certainly get to dust off his tux.

In the stuffy room, not every reporter wore a jacket. Gordon had ditched his long ago to the back of his chair next to his brand-new desk near the window. Next to Gordon stood, Jack Hanson, an older man with a wife and three kids, needed more deodorant. His body odor wafted around him like a fog. Gordon eased away from Hanson under a false presence, all the while wondering how the older reporter had three kids.

"I'm gonna get that top story," Johnny Flynn said to Gordon. Shorter than Gordon by at least four inches, Johnny nonetheless had an effortless aplomb. His charm and good looks opened a lot of doors and he nearly always had his tie cinched tight. "And I'll get the next promotion by, you know, actually writing something that's true."

Johnny still hadn't accepted the fact that Gordon had received a promotion for fabricating a news story. To him, you wrote and then you accepted the accolades. What made matters even worse for Gordon was that he couldn't say anything about the nature of the story. For all Johnny knew, Gordon's story was about a bank robbery foiled by the police. The real story involved Nazis in Houston. As a result, he had to suffer Johnny's tirades and one-upmanship.

Gordon hated it. But he loved his desk next to the window so when Johnny got a little too full of himself, Gordon would just saunter over to his desk and stretch out while Johnny had to content himself with a small hovel in the middle of the newsroom.

"Don't talk about stuff you don't know a damn thing about," Gordon whispered. He nodded to their boss.

"Y'all done?" Levitz asked. His cocked eyebrow spoke volumes.

Both junior reporters nodded.

Levitz sniggered. "There'll be no switching. You get what you get and you won't throw a fit."

What was this, kindergarten?

"Harry," Levitz said, "got a dime?"

Harry Vinson plunged his hand into his pocket and produced the coin.

"Now, since Johnny here wrote the last big piece for us, I'm gonna let him call it. What's it gonna be, Johnny?"

"Heads."

Harry flipped the coin. "Tails."

The grin on Gordon's face could've lit up the marquee at the Metropolitan movie house. "I'll take…"

"Not so fast, Gordie." Levitz used the nickname Gordon typically despised, a fact the editor knew and exploited. "You only get the right to choose the slip of paper. Left hand or right hand."

Again, Gordon thought, Is this kindergarten? He wanted the story of the dead artist. Marie Gardner, his mother, taught art at Sam Houston High School and was part of the committee that helped found and open Houston's Museum of Fine Arts. Gordon knew he could make William Silber's obit shine.

Being right-handed, Gordon's natural tendency was to pick right. But he had been under Levitz's black cloud for a few weeks. Sure, Gordon had successfully bartered his silence for the new desk and promotion, something Levitz had agreed to under pressure. But the editor didn't like having his hand forced and had rewarded Gordon with lesser stories. The last high-profile story Gordon got still only landed on page two. To date, the only page-one story Gordon had was the fake story he had written.

"Left," Gordon said.

"Good choice. You get the crazy man."

Gordon's pained sigh brought chuckles from the guys around him.

"Johnny, you get Silber," Levitz said. "All right, boys, let's make some ink."

As the throng dispersed, Gordon moved against the

stream toward Levitz. "Wait, boss. I'm better for the artist profile. I know more than Johnny does."

Johnny, who remained in place as the reporters and photographers moved past him, just watched.

"Don't care." Levitz turned to Barbara and motioned her to follow him. He threw the two pieces of paper in the trash can and sequestered himself in his office.

She gave Gordon a sympathetic look. "Sorry, sweetie." She straightened her skirt and joined Levitz, closing his door.

Gordon shook his head and caught a glimpse of Johnny. Now his rival wore the marquee-bright grin. He turned and sauntered away.

Frowning, Gordon fished out the two pieces of paper Levitz had thrown away. He looked at each of them.

Both pieces of paper were blank.

CHAPTER TWO

The Houston Police Department was a stuffy place filled with the stink of cigarette smoke, stale body odor, and the aftershave that tried to mask it but failed. The large room with pairs of desks butted up against each other resembled a newsroom.

Gordon smiled and shook hands with many of the detectives and cops. Early on when covering the crime beat, Gordon had started putting the names of the officers in his stories. He discovered these guys loved seeing their names in print. More than a few would actually cut out the stories and pin them to bulletin boards. For a few of the younger officers, having their names mentioned by Gordon Gardner was a rite of passage.

Of course, Gordon had an ulterior motive for all this glad-handing: it made the lips of these officers a little more pliable for off-the-record comments and background. And when those younger officers got promotions, Gordon had his in.

"Hiya, Burt." Gordon came up behind a big man sitting at a desk and patted his shoulder. "How's life treating you?" He slid into the seat next to the desk.

Gordon didn't see his playful tap slosh coffee onto the fuzzy mustache of Detective Burt Wheeler. A burly man whose girth was more than intimidating, Burt put his cup back on the table and wiped his mouth with a handkerchief. Then he mopped the sweat from his brow. "I don't like wearing coffee, Gordie. Watch it next time."

Palms up, Gordon said, "Message received." He tipped his hat back on his head. "Whatcha know?"

Burt indicated the stack of files on his desk. "That I haven't seen the top of my desk for a week."

"I heard you caught the crazy guy who jumped in front of a car. So, the scoop?"

Burt started ruffling through the stacks of paper on his desk. "Do me a favor? Leave my name off this'un, huh? Too weird."

"Spill." Gardner pulled out a notebook and got his pencil ready.

"You probably won't need that." Burt leaned back in his chair and lit a cigarette. "Story's too short. Ain't even sure how you gonna fill up your inches."

Gordon smirked. "I'll embellish."

Taking a deep pull on the cigarette, Burt told the story. "The stiff's name is Victor Tompkins, thirty-one. He's a door-to-door salesman selling encyclopedias. Like anybody but a library would want those."

"Tut tut, my good man," Gordon said, imitating a British accent. "A learned man is one who makes good decisions."

"Then our victim didn't read what he was selling. Witnesses say he was talking loudly about phantom automobiles, how there was a car out to get him. He supposedly was acting really crazy, talking about proving the vehicle was a ghost. That's when he stepped out into the street and got slammed to the ground." Burt clapped his hands in imitation of the body being hit by a speeding car.

"Death was fast? Did the victim say anything?"

"Nope. Well maybe 'Guess I was wrong.'"

"The eyewitnesses, you got a list?"

"Yeah, but it's small. Hairdresser lady was outside taking a smoke break, gas station attendants were only half looking in the right direction, and some folks walking down the street who decided to stay and talk with the responding officers. Nothing much, really."

Burt found the file and opened it, letting Gordon copy down the names of the witnesses. "Thanks for all the tips, Burt."

"Don't mention it. And don't mention it was me that caught this one, okay?"

"Why the hot potato?"

Burt scowled and looked around the room.

Gordon followed and took in only what you'd expect to see in a police station: a room full of detectives and cops, some on phones talking, others in small clusters chatting, still others with their heads down buried in paperwork.

"Okay," Burt said, conspiratorially, "this is definitely off the record."

Gordon complied by putting his pencil and pad into his inside jacket pocket. "Shoot."

"Tompkins, the victim," Burt began, still looking around the room. "See he came in a few times yakking about seeing things."

Gordon fought the urge to pull his pad and pencil

back out. "Things? What kinds of things?"

"All sorts. Said there were spirits only he could see, flying around his neighborhood. He even saw them in his house. Said there were a few here in the station when he came in to make a complaint."

Gordon leaned in. "What kinds of complaint?"

"The usual stuff from paranoid wackos like him. Said he thought there were people following him, said he saw a UFO flying outside of town on one of his trips, you know, stuff like that."

Gordon shrugged. "Anything legit?"

"Nah. We get little old ladies calling about hooey like that all the time. We just don't have the manpower to follow up on every claim. When Tompkins came in doing the same, we just chalked it up to paranoia. Maybe all that time alone, driving and talking with strangers, reading his books made his mind wander. Or maybe he read too many of them pulp magazines."

Inwardly, Gordon smiled. He knew exactly the kinds of pulp magazines Burt was talking about. On the side, and using a pen name, Gordon was an avid writer of pulp tales, having submitted over three dozen to various magazines over the years. He'd had only marginal success but he still kept at it. In fact, listening to Burt's retelling of the strange circumstances surrounding Victor Tompkins, Gordon's literary imagination was already starting to churn.

Gordon gave Burt a misdirect. "How many times did he come in?"

Burt shrugged. "Not sure. While we're supposed to

keep all records, sometimes they find their way to the trash can. Three, four times, maybe."

"And the last time?"

"About two weeks ago. And here's the catch: guess what he was complaining about?"

"The high price of tea in China?"

"Nice, but no. He was scared because he swore there was a car following him."

CHAPTER THREE

Elmer Magee looked exactly like the kind of person you'd find working as a county coroner. He was short, skinny, with round glasses covering eyes that appeared too close together, as if all his intense gazing at the body parts of dead people had somehow moved his eyes closer to his nose. His shirt sleeves were wrinkled and his tie was loosened. The apron he wore over his clothes was splashed with various liquids.

He wiped his hands on a clean towel and looked at Gordon. The reporter had the sudden urge to wave his hand in front of Elmer's face to verify he could see.

"Elmer, how's my favorite coroner?" From his pocket, Gordon produced a pack of clove cigarettes. He tossed the pack to Elmer who caught it.

"Bodies piled high and three days behind schedule," came the reply. His voiced matched his look: squeaky, like he was still going through puberty. "Do you realize the DA actually thinks I can expedite an autopsy? I mean a scalpel can only cut as fast as the hand of the coroner. We're understaffed, overworked, and I barely see the sun anymore except on weekends."

"I'll put in a good word to the sun on your behalf when I leave, make sure it doesn't rain on your next day off."

"You are many things, Gordon, but a master of the weather you're not. Who are you here to visit? I've got some new ones: an apparent suicide, a dead artist, a construction worker who lost a battle with a power drill. Oh, and the car guy."

"Car guy?"

"The jumper who got smashed by a car."

"That's mine." Gordon was tempted to ask about the artist, perhaps even get Elmer to reveal some details as far as he knew them. But, no, his Methodist minister father wouldn't have approved. Gordon was going to keep his edge on Johnny Flynn, but he was going to do it fair and square. "Detective Wheeler tells me he was raving about phantom cars and such, then jumped in front of one."

"I don't worry about all that. I just deal with facts. And the fact is Mr. Tompkins was hit by a speeding car. And suffered multiple contusions and broken bones. Both lungs were punctured and he bled out internally. Preliminary diagnosis is that he drowned in his own fluids."

"Is that all?" Gordon asked sardonically. He scribbled in his note pad.

"You wanna see him?"

"Not particularly. You crack open the skull?"

"Not any more so than was already done by the ground. Why?"

"Cops say the victim filed a report about seeing things and such. Didn't know if he had a tumor or something that would explain it."

Elmer shook his head. "From what I could tell, his brain was normal. Didn't crack him open all the way. No reason. And, without any authorization from the family,

I won't. They're already asking when they can have the body."

"Really? That usual?"

"More or less. Depends. Sometimes it's a religious thing, sometimes the family wants the death certificate to hurry up the probate process and get the inheritance."

Gordon made a note to check on the family. "Let me ask you something: medically speaking, what would make a man think there are phantom cars so much so that he'd jump in front of one to prove or disprove the point?"

Elmer snapped his fingers. "I was waiting for someone to ask me that."

"Didn't Wheeler?"

"Nope. I don't think he cares. He just wants the clearance."

Gordon spread his hands. "Well, doctor, enlighten me."

Elmer's smile froze in his face. He faltered slightly. "I can't. We'll, I can't yet. You see, I thought the victim might've been drunk or on some kind of medication. So I took some of his blood and sent it to a lab that'll do some tests on it. That way, we'll see if he was high as a kite or just crazy."

"How long?"

"Days, most likely." He shrugged sheepishly. "When's the story run?"

"Tomorrow."

Elmer winced. "Cripes. Well, let me make a call."

Gordon patted the smaller man on the shoulder. "Thanks, Elmer. I'll be sure to drop your name in the piece."

CHAPTER FOUR

The spot where Victor Tompkins lost his challenge with a car was west of downtown at the intersection of Washington and Sawyer, two blocks south of the major westbound railroad. In his notebook, Gordon drew a crude map of the crime scene with Washington as the east/west street and Sawyer the north/south. In the northwest quadrant, he wrote "doctor's office." "Gas station" was in the northeast side while "Betsy's Beauty Salon" filled the southeast area. For the southwest side, he wrote "Jake's Diner." There was a bus stop in front of the beauty shop. It was in this area that Tompkins leapt in front of the passing car.

Gordon entered the salon. A bell signaled his arrival. All the women, both the beauticians and the patrons in chairs, turned to look his way. Even the old women sitting under the hair dryers put down their magazines and looked at him.

Removing his hat, Gordon put on his million-dollar smile. "Morning, ladies. It's a fine day out, isn't it?"

"It is," said a beautician with blond hair swept up on top of her head. She looked at him over her glasses, then back down to her client's hair. She made an extra snip. "What can we do for you?"

"My name's Gordon Gardner. I'm a reporter for the *Post-Dispatch*. I'm writing a story on the man who got hit by the car out in front of your store. I'd like to talk with anyone here who might've witnessed it."

The clamor of voices that erupted all at once from everyone in the salon made Gordon jump back a step. His million-dollar smile dropped to a hundred grand as he took out his notebook. "I'm sorry, ladies, but could I have it one at a time, perhaps with some corroboration along the way?"

The blonde put her scissors down and wiped her hands. "I'll tell you exactly what happened."

"And you are?"

"Betsy Beadilia. I'm the owner. As it happened in front of my salon, I'll be the one who speaks."

Gordon moved to the window and gazed at the small group of people waiting for the bus. "Looks like y'all had a front row seat."

Betsy came and stood next to him. Her perfume was light and elegant, a fragrance that matched her supple, strong hands. "You're not kidding. I have a rule in here that no one smokes. Ruins the atmosphere. I was outside taking a smoke break when I heard the crazy man."

"Why'd you think he was crazy?"

Her look indicated she thought Gordon was crazy. "If a man starts shouting about cars vanishing into thin air and cars following people, don't you think that sounds a little crazy?" The more Betsy talked, the more her East Texas accent emerged. She managed to convert the word "air" into two syllables.

"I see your point. So, tell me, what happened?"

Betsy turned to the other women. "Y'all tell me if I get something wrong, 'kay?" Heads bobbed up and down.

The other beauticians stopped their jobs and settled in to listen.

"It was just a few days ago, Saturday it was. We were busy all day long. I had to call in Charlene on her day off to come in and do manicures. People were out and about and the bus stop was full of people. A normal Saturday, right?"

"As rain." Gordon alternatively looked into Betsy's deep green eyes and his notebook.

"So, even though we turned on the radio and opened the windows, we still could hear this strange ranting. I stepped outside to smoke and get a look at what was going on. I walked out and Dottie Ballard came out with me. She's off today or else she would tell you the same thing. Any chance we can get her name in the paper?"

"Sure thing." Gordon wrote Dottie's name in the notebook. "So the two of y'all are outside and Mr. Tompkins starts, what, talking about ghost cars?"

"*Phantom* cars," said Betsy and a few other women, almost in unison. "He specifically used that word. He said the phantom cars disappeared into thin air only to come back and follow him."

Gordon frowned. "This thin air thing, any clue what that was?"

"No. But he yelled loud enough to attract attention from just about everyone."

"So he was waiting for the bus?"

"That's when I saw him, yes," Betsy said. "And then he jumped, saying he was going to prove to everyone that the car wasn't real."

"And then it really hit him," one of the other women said. "It was a dreadful sound, too. Like when my husband hit a deer while going hunting."

Up until that point, Gordon had pretty much known most of the details. Now for something new. "What kind of car?"

"Black," said Betsy. "Ford, Model 48, four-door. 1936 or 1937, I think."

"Know cars, do you?" Gordon added one more thing to the ledger of Betsy's qualities. "I drive a Lincoln Zephyr myself. Best car I ever owned."

"How many have you owned?"

"One." He waggled his eyebrows. "What happened to the driver?"

"Got banged up. Had the ambulance come and take him to the hospital. Not sure if the police charged him or not."

"Not that I've heard. The victim, Mr. Tompkins. Did he say anything after he was hit?"

Betsy looked away toward the spot in the street where the body had lain. She seemed to grow distant with the memory. "Not a word. Just lay there in his own blood and died."

***

Gordon took his leave of the women with new insights into the death of Victor Tompkins. He stood in front of the beauty salon and gazed at the intersection. What was Tompkins doing here? He was obviously waiting for a bus, but how did he get here? Gordon figured he must have taken a cab or another bus to get to this spot.

He decided to canvass the three other businesses on the theory that the same events viewed from different angles might reveal something new. Jake's Diner was first. They were gearing up for the lunch hour rush so the joint was hopping. Jake himself, all five-foot-nine of him, stepped out from behind the counter, wiping his hands on an already dirty towel.

"Nah, I didn't see it. I was working. Heard about it when all my customers started lookin' out the window. Even the wait staff stopped to gawk. It was a pain in the ass, too, because some little piss-ant got sick and vomited his lunch. Had to give him a damn refund."

***

The front door of the doctor's office faced away from the line of sight of the accident. Only a side window gave a direct view. The shingle hanging from the door read "Dr. Kermit Kernow, Ph. D."

No bell announced Gordon's entry but a pleasant-looking secretary looked up from her typing. Her pleasant smile matched her pleasant clothes. "Good morning. May I help you?"

Gordon only gave her a thousand-dollar smile. He didn't want to outshine her. "Gordon Gardner, *Post-Dispatch*. I'm writing a story on last Saturday's accident. Is Doctor Kernow in?" He pronounced the word to rhyme with the word 'low.'

"Kernow," the secretary said. "It sounds like 'now.'"

"Right. So, about the man who got hit? Was he a

patient here?"

"I'm afraid I can't say, Mr. Gardner. Why do you ask?"

Gordon shrugged. "I'm canvassing the businesses at this corner, seeing maybe why he was here. He didn't get his hair done at Betsy's, he didn't eat at Jake's Diner, he was on foot so he didn't need any gas. That leaves y'all."

"Well, if he was a patient here, it would be the doctor's prerogative to reveal anything."

"Well, that's just nice and tidy, isn't it?" Gordon put his notebook back into his pocket. "Was Mr. Tompkins scheduled for a visit that morning?"

"I couldn't say."

"Couldn't or won't?"

"Won't." The smile never left her lips.

"The doctor in? I'd like to speak with him."

"He is, but he's with a client."

Stymied, Gordon asked again. "So you can't tell me if the victim had an appointment the day he died or if he was even a patient?"

"Precisely."

"I could infer." He let the notion linger in the air.

"And you might be liable." None of the joviality left her face.

"Right. Well, good day. Thank you for your time." He turned and put his hat back on his head.

Outside, Gordon stared at the doctor's office. He was

stunned. That was the kind of business he usually dished out. He wasn't used to being on the receiving end of it. Was that just an overprotective secretary or was there something here?

Gordon walked across the street to the gas station. The attendants all clustered around the reporter and corroborated most of what he already knew. Only when he glanced back across the street to Dr. Kernow's office did he notice two things.

The first was that the doctor's window faced in this direction, toward the intersection and accident site. The secretary had no way of knowing for sure whether the doctor saw anything.

The second thing he noticed was that someone was looking out the window at that very moment, staring directly at him.

CHAPTER FIVE

The address from Victor Tompkins's driver's license indicated he lived on the near east side of downtown off Polk Street. When Gordon pulled up in front of the house, a couple of things piqued his curiosity. One, was the house itself. It was an older house, probably forty years old. The distinctive turn-of-the-century vibe from the architecture made him wonder if Tompkins liked antiques. The second thing that surprised him more was that the house was still occupied.

Wheeler hadn't bothered to tell Gordon about any background on Tompkins—"he's a dead guy in the street hit by a car. It's a shame, but there's no case here." As Gordon approached the front door, he legitimately wondered who was in the house.

He checked his watch and made sure he had time for this excursion. In an hour he was due to meet Bruno Clavell for their initial interview.

Peeling paint flecked off the door when Gordon rapped the old wood with his knuckles. The porch boards creaked under his weight and he didn't think anyone should sit in the dilapidated porch swing. Try as he might, he couldn't help forming notions of the type of man Tompkins was.

When the door opened, a woman of about forty looked out. She appeared haggard, with dark rings under her eyes. Her blouse was wrinkled and she wore a faded blue skirt. Her feet were bare. "Can I help you?"

He tipped his hat to her. "Gordon Gardner, Mrs. Tompkins, I work for the *Post-Dispatch*. I'm writing a story on your husband's death."

She chuckled dryly. "My husband's still alive, Mr. Gardner. And I'm not Mrs. Tompkins. I'm Victor's sister. For a reporter, you ought to get your facts straight."

"My apologies. The good folks at the police department didn't have a lot of information for me."

She shrugged. "They don't care about Vic. Did you say you're writing a story about him?"

"I am."

She narrowed her eyes. "Why?"

"Because he died in such a way that the public is curious. We'd like to set the record straight."

"What needs straightening? He was hit by a car crossing the street."

Gordon opened his mouth but paused a moment before speaking. "Ma'am, what did the police tell you?"

"They told me he stepped out into the street and was hit by some man driving too fast."

"Did they mention that many eyewitnesses claimed they heard him talk about, well, they said he thought the car wasn't real."

The woman visibly slumped. "You'd better come inside." She stepped back and opened the door. Gordon entered, removing his hat.

If the exterior needed painting, the interior was quite the opposite. Everything inside was neat and orderly.

Doilies covered almost every horizontal surface, area rugs did the same for the hardwood floors, and the scent of jasmine filled the air. Gordon followed Victor's sister. *Why on earth would someone as young as Victor live in a house like this?* He rounded a corner and found his answer.

The woman sitting in a wingback chair had to be at least eighty-five, maybe even ninety. She was thin and frail, her house dress lying limp on bony shoulders. Her white hair was pulled back in a bun that sat on the lower part of her head. The thick glasses she wore magnified her eyes so much that she looked bug-eyed. Next to her chair was a small table on which sat yet another doily, a row of medicine bottles, a magnifying glass, a folded newspaper open to the crossword puzzle, and a glass of water.

"Mr. Gardner, this is my mother, Gertrude Tompkins. My brother lived here with her and took care of her. My name's Naomi Wilson, by the way." She extended her hand. Gordon shook it before turning his attention to the elderly woman.

"Good morning, Mrs. Tompkins." He knelt so she didn't have to look up.

"What in the devil are you doing on the floor, Victor?" she asked. "Stand up."

Gordon and Naomi exchanged a glance. Her expression was unreadable. He stood and sat in the chair opposite the elderly woman.

Naomi sat in a chair next to her mother. "Mom,"— she talked loudly and slowly—"this is a reporter from the paper." She tapped the open crossword puzzle. "The paper. He's here about Victor."

"Is Victor home yet?" Gertrude asked, looking at her daughter.

"No, Mom, he's not. Remember, he's gone. He died."

The old woman's eyes opened wider, surprise creeping into them. "No, he's not. He left on another business trip last Friday. He said he needed to head back up the road to an old prospect and try again." She spoke with utter clarity and conviction.

Naomi frowned. "Right, Mom, but he had an accident. I told you he had an accident."

Gertrude opened her mouth in a small o. "No, that nice man told me about Victor."

Gordon pulled out his notebook. "What man?"

"The nice man with the suit. I'm not sure who he was. He told me he was a friend of Victor's. I hadn't seen him before Saturday."

Again, Gordon and Naomi exchanged looks. "Are you sure it was Saturday, Mom?"

"Oh yes. I was listening to Edgar Bergen and Charlie McCarthy on the radio when he arrived." She turned and patted the large radio next to her chair. "It took me a while to get to the door, but he was there when I opened it."

"And you had never seen him before?" Gordon said.

"No, I hadn't. Victor doesn't have many friends on account of his job. He's a traveling salesman, you know."

"Yes, ma'am."

"And he reads those encyclopedias. He's a real smart cracker, my Victor. And he loves me so much that he stays with me."

Now Gordon knew why the house felt like a time capsule.

He scooted to the edge of his chair. "Mrs. Tompkins, what did the man want?"

"He was a friend of Victor's, you see," the old lady repeated herself. "He said that Victor sent him here to the house to pick up a few things. Victor was going to stay longer out on the road. I was surprised since Victor's room has a lock on the door and only Victor has the key."

Gordon glanced at Naomi for confirmation. "Yes," she said. "It was Victor's only stipulation when he and I and our older sister agreed that the best thing for Mom was for one of us to live with her. He gave up his own apartment to come back and live in his old room. He said that if he was going to give up his freedom, he still needed a place all to his own."

"And have you gone in there since Saturday?"

She shook her head. "The police haven't released his effects yet. The key's still with them."

Gordon arched an eyebrow and stood. "Would you excuse us, Mrs. Tompkins?" He nodded towards the kitchen and motioned for Naomi to follow.

"Do you have any idea who this mystery man was?" he asked her.

"Not at all. It's true that Victor didn't have many friends come over. When they did, they'd usually set out back on the porch and talked or played cards while Mom stayed inside. Why?"

Gordon put a finger to his lips. "I'm just wondering aloud here. Who would come by the house looking to go into Victor's room on the very day Victor was killed?"

Naomi shrugged. "I don't have any idea."

Biting his lip, Gordon hesitated before asking the next question. "Would you mind if I tried to open the door?"

"How?"

He sighed. "I have a friend. He's a private investigator and, well, he's shown me how to pick locks." He let a few beats of silence rest.

"Sure, if you want to try. Can't hurt. Only other way in is the window."

She led Gordon back through the house to the rearmost room. Like a salesman, Naomi presented the door to him. He knelt and examined the knob.

It was a common indoor lock that only needed a thin rod to be inserted into the hole. For those who knew how, it was a simple lock.

Reaching into his pocket, Gardner pulled out a pocket knife and turned it over in his hands. "This little gadget was made in Switzerland." He showed it to Naomi. "It's not just a pocket knife, but multiple tools. This one's modified with a straight piece,"—he used a fingernail and extended a metal rod from the pack—"specifically for what we're trying to do."

Again, he crouched and slipped the rod into the small hole. With a little flick of his wrist, the lock clicked open.

He stood and stepped back, letting Naomi open the door.

"That's quite a trick for a reporter," she said.

"I don't often do it, but when I do, it's always for a good reason."

She turned the knob and opened the door. Both were instantly aware of the draft in the room.

They walked in and saw the source. The raised window was shattered, glass pieces scattered all over the floor.

"Oh my." Naomi walked over to the window, then remembered she was barefoot. She looked at the floor, then up at Gordon.

"How bad is your mother's hearing?" Gordon asked.

"Pretty much gone. When she listens to the radio, she's got to turn it up pretty loud."

What surprised them both was the condition of the room. It was all but untouched except for the broken window.

"Is this how his room normally was?" Gordon asked.

"Pretty much. I've been in here a few times."

"Can you tell if anything's missing?"

She gazed around the room. The twin bed and the little side table, sans doily, sat across from the window. The bed was rumpled, but made. A bookcase flanked the wall next to the window and a chair was positioned next to the armoire. There was a small desk off in the corner and Gordon looked it over. There were sales receipts and itineraries.

His toe bumped something metallic under the desk. Upon closer inspection, it turned out to be a cash box. Judging by its weight, it was full.

"That's odd," Gordon said. "A break-in but the cash box is still here."

"I think I know what's missing," Naomi said. She pointed to the table next to the bed. There was an empty glass and a small notepad. She held up the pad for Gordon to read.

Across the top were listed the days of the week. Under each date were marks, three each for each day. At the bottom of the page, Victor had written "10 mg daily."

"What kind of medicine was he taking?" Gordon asked.

"I'm not sure, but all the bottles are gone."

CHAPTER SIX

Gordon Gardner's mind raced with the possibilities and their meanings as he drove his Lincoln Zephyr across town to the Plaza Apartment Hotel. He wanted to keep the momentum focused on the new wrinkle in the Tompkins story, but he had an interview to conduct with Bruno Clavell, the second story assigned to him.

Another glance at his watch. He was going to be late. Talking with Naomi about the ramifications of apparently stolen medicine had taken longer than he expected. She wondered if she should call the police. The bark of laughter that erupted out of him made him suddenly embarrassed.

"If they don't care enough to even let me know about your brother's living arrangements," Gordon had said, "I'm pretty sure they're not going to care about some stolen pills."

"But what kind of medicine was he taking," Naomi had asked, "that someone would want to break in and steal them?"

"That is a very good question."

The kind of question that demanded an immediate follow up from Dr. Kernow himself. But Gordon couldn't do it now. When he had been assigned to do a write-up on Bruno Clavell and his new nightclub, Gordon became excited. He loved music and dancing and frequented the various dance halls at least once a week. The Clavell Club was the latest in a string of similar nightclubs all across Texas. The price for a ticket to the gala was going to be higher than most so a free pass inside the club was something to strive for. Or work for, as was the case for Gordon that night.

Those were his final thoughts on that story as the Plaza came into view. Situated at the corner of Montrose Boulevard and Bartlett Street, the Plaza was built in 1926 and modeled after the Ritz-Carlton in New York. The eight-floor, brown-bricked structure had two wings jutting off a central axis. In a city with an ever increasing number of fancy places, the Plaza was among the fanciest.

Knowing the paper wouldn't cover the cost of valet parking, Gordon parked along Bartlett and walked to the lobby. He gave the concierge his name and waited while a call was placed up to Clavell's rooms. With a grin that barely registered on the smile scale, the concierge directed Gordon to the elevator.

The elevator doors opened and the attendant gave the reporter a broad smile. "Good afternoon, sir. What floor?"

"Seven," Gordon said. "Bruno Clavell's floor."

"Yes, sir." The attendant was an old Negro with a name tag that read "Moses."

"How are you getting along today, Moses?" Gordon asked. He made it a point, in his reporting career, to talk to all the service personnel he could. Often, they knew the best secrets because the people they serviced typically ignored them.

"Fine, sir, very fine." Moses stood while he operated the elevator. A folded newspaper lay on the thin stool where Moses sat during down times.

"*Chronicle* or *Post-Dispatch*?" Gordon asked.

"*Chronicle*," Moses replied.

"You'll have to buy the *Post* to read my article," Gordon said. "I'm doing a write-up on Mr. Clavell."

"Yes, sir. But you'll have to get the *Chronicle* to read their story on Mr. Clavell."

Gordon frowned. "Have they been here already?"

"Come and gone, sir." The bell chimed and Moses activated the door. "Seventh floor. Mr. Clavell's room is at the end." He smiled.

Gordon, momentarily surprised, shuffled down the hall to the last room. He knocked and waited. A moment later, the door opened and a man appeared in the frame. Gordon tipped his hat and introduced himself. The man glanced at his watch. "You're late." He stepped back and allowed Gordon to enter.

The suite was spacious and luxurious, one of the four-room types throughout the hotel. The window faced northeast, giving Clavell a good view of downtown Houston.

Bruno Clavell was tall, a shade over six feet, with his hair perfectly coiffed in the latest style. Even at this hour of the day, he was impeccably dressed in a tan suit and green tie. His shoes were shined to perfection.

"You didn't bring a photographer?" Clavell sat and motioned Gordon to a chair opposite him.

"No, sir." Gordon took off his hat and placed it brim up on the couch. He sat in a comfortable chair and brought out his notebook. "The photographer will be there tonight at the grand opening. I'm here for your story."

Clavell grunted. "The *Chronicle* reporter brought his camera man. Got a picture of me here in my rooms."

Gordon thought back to his discussion with his editor. Levitz told Gordon to get Clavell's story first, even when specifically asked about bringing along a photographer. "I'm not running a show-and-tell on the Plaza," Levitz had said. "Most people don't care about that. They just want to know about the man behind all these fancy clubs."

Well, thought Gordon, *strike one for Levitz's acumen*. The question Gordon really wanted to ask was the name of the *Chronicle* reporter. Few rival reporters intimidated Gordon Gardner, but he at least liked to know his competition. To Clavell, he said, "We can circle back later today, if you like, but it's our opinion that most people want to have a look inside your club. It's an exclusive ticket tonight. Who all is supposed to be here?"

The change in Clavell's face was immediate. He softened his countenance as he spoke, beaming with pride. "Benny Goodman and his orchestra are here. Joel McCrea's in town. So is Gene Autry. Shirley Temple phoned but she's not old enough. Our biggest surprise is Myrna Loy and William Powell, Mr. and Mrs. Thin Man themselves."

"Nice," Gordon murmured, writing down all the names. "How'd you manage that?"

"My line of nightclubs across Texas has become *the* destinations for night life. Houston was the last major city in Texas we needed to conquer before we go national.

We already have plans for New Orleans, St. Louis, and Memphis. The Clavell Clubs feature the latest in luxury and entertainment. All the top touring orchestras want to play our clubs. The stars, when they travel through Texas, make it a point to be seen visiting one of my clubs."

Gordon's pencil flew across the pages as Clavell spoke about his life, his stint working in a jazz ensemble touring Europe, and how he opened his first nightclub. It was all very effective. Clavell definitely had the telling of his story down to a science. It was no wonder he was among the up-and-coming celebrities in the field.

"And the best and brightest here in Houston will be there tonight. Businessmen, socialites, lawyers, doctors, actors, sport stars—it'll be the biggest event in Houston's history."

One thing caught in Gordon's mind. "Do you happen to have a guest list I can use and pull out the top names for the story?"

Clavell arched an eyebrow. "You are going to be there tonight, are you not?"

"Yes."

"Do you have a tuxedo?"

"Of course."

Clavell thought for a moment, and then rose. He strode across the room to a desk and shuffled through some papers. Finding what he was looking for, he showed it to Gordon who had come to stand next to the nightclub owner.

Gordon took the papers and reviewed them. He

moved over to the kitchen table and wrote down a few of the major names: Jesse H. Jones, Governor W. Lee O'Daniel, and Mayor Oscar Holcombe.

One name caught his eye: Dr. Kermit Kernow.

Well, looks like I'll get to ask my questions after all.

CHAPTER SEVEN

"Are you kidding me?" Gordon's voice rose with exasperation. "You want me to write the story now? I don't even have all the facts."

Eli Levitz stared at his reporter over his reading glasses. "Did the guy jump in front of the car?"

"Yes, but..."

"Did he get hit?"

"Yes, but..."

"Did he die of his sustained injuries?"

"Yes, but he…"

"There you go. There's your story." He tapped his watch. "You got thirty minutes."

"But what about all the eyewitnesses claiming Tompkins was ranting about phantom automobiles?"

Levitz cantered his head. "Why do we care what crazy people say before they do crazy things?"

"Because there's something more here, Eli. I can feel it."

Levitz rubbed his stomach. "I can feel my ulcer coming on if we keep talking."

Gordon snapped his fingers. "The pills. What about the theft of the pills?"

The editor tapped his pencil against the desk blotter. "You said the old lady was deaf as a board. So what that someone swiped the pills? Doesn't have any bearing on the fact that your victim intentionally jumped in front of a moving car and lost."

"Because he was taking those pills."

"You don't know that," Levitz shot back, "and you've got no way to prove it. But what you do have is four inches of space to fill with content. Now get to it before you go to your big shindig tonight." Levitz leaned back in his chair. "And don't get under Clavell's skin like you did before."

Gordon frowned. "What do you mean?"

"I heard you rubbed him the wrong way, that's all."

"Where'd you hear that?"

"It just filtered down from upstairs, and that's all I'm going to say about that." Levitz didn't have to go any further. All reporters, copy boys, typists, and artists knew what "upstairs" meant. Robert G. Preston, III, the owner of the paper. He was connected all throughout the city and had his finger on the pulse of his paper. He let the various editors run the show, but would stick his nose in if he thought he could do anything.

Gordon nodded, scowling. "Got it. Who's doing photog with me?"

Levitz visibly brightened. "New gal. Lucy Barnes. Comes highly recommended from Dallas. Even had a spread in Time last year. Vogue, too." Vogue, in recent years, had begun to use more photography in its magazine rather than the traditional illustrations, something that helped cause the demise and merger of rival Vanity Fair.

Gordon stood. "Why not Jimmy or Steve or Harry? They're all good."

"And they're all men. The Chronicle's sending over a pair of guys tonight. We're going with something different. You and she are going to wade out into high society and capture Bruno Clavell in his element. Think of it as a high-class safari. Who knows? You might even capture one. Just don't mount them to your wall." Levitz slammed his palms on the desk and stood. "Now, go get me my four inches on the jump and be done with it before you leave." He snapped his fingers. "You've got a tux, right?"

"Yeah, yeah, I got a blasted tux," Gordon said, "and I've even convinced the moths to take a vacation. How do you know the Chronicle's sending over a couple of guys?"

"Because they both went to Clavell's apartment."

"Right. Speaking of that, why didn't we send over a cameraman with me?"

Levitz lit a cigarette. "Because we didn't think it was necessary. We're a newspaper, for Pete's sake. We report the news."

Gordon grinned. "So Clavell called and complained."

"Like a little girl. So, we're going to one-up the Chronicle and send you out with a lady. Clavell's sure to forget our little misstep when he catches sight of the two of y'all."

Something in the way Levitz spoke those words made Gordon square his shoulders. He straightened his tie. "Where is she?"

"Getting her orders from Jack. You'll meet her later. Now go write the damn story so I can print it."

Gordon returned to his original reason for coming into the office. "Eli, I'm telling you there's something more here."

"And I'm telling you it all adds up to a crime beat story you ain't even gonna have your name on so get your rear over to your desk and write the damn piece." He blew smoke through his lips and stabbed his half-finished cigarette in the overflowing ash tray.

Gordon knew when to back off. He nodded and slipped out of the room, closing the door behind him. He stopped at Barbara Essary's desk. The editor's secretary was typing up a memo. On the side of her desk were two baskets, one for incoming copy Levitz needed to review and one for stories with the editor's changes marked that the typists would correct.

The top of the stack of already-reviewed stories was one by Johnny Flynn. It was the other story he had been assigned, the one on the rumors that local businessman Jesse H. Jones might be tapped by President Roosevelt to be Secretary of Commerce. Only a few marks were on the nearly clean copy.

Gordon started leafing through the stack before Betty slapped his hand. "Get outta there, Gordon. You know better than that."

"Yeah, I know. I was looking for Johnny's other story, his crime beat one."

She looked up at him, her blue eyes sparkling. "It's not turned in yet. He convinced the boss there was something more going on. The artist, William Silber, was up to something since he was killed in a part of town he didn't normally frequent. Johnny's got another day."

Gordon shook his head. "Figures." He bit his lip, wondering if there was a way to slow down Johnny's rise. He was just going to have to console himself by sitting in his big desk next to the window. "This new girl, the photographer Mr. Levitz paired me up with for the Clavell story, you seen her?"

"Yeah, sweetie, I've seen her. We powdered our noses in the same ladies room. I've even seen her work. She'll be a nice addition to the paper if she stays."

"If she stays?"

"Yeah. This story is like a tryout. The big boss likes her, he'll give her a job. If not, well, she'll just move on to another opportunity." She tapped the basket with the incoming stories still waiting for Levitz's review. "He'll need your story before your big party tonight. I'm so jealous."

Gordon glanced at the near pristine copy of Johnny Flynn's story and stifled his own kind of jealousy.

CHAPTER EIGHT

Levitz's big plan was for Gordon and Lucy to arrive together, more like they were a couple attending the gala rather than a couple of reporters. "Those *Chronicle* bums are gonna look like a pair of squares showing up together. When y'all walk in, they won't know y'all are reporters. Sure, when she starts snapping pictures, they might have an idea, but they'll forget all that and just be dazzled by her looks."

When Levitz had said that, Gordon's imagination had run wild. He'd known and dated plenty of beautiful women, but Levitz had been married twenty years. Perhaps his standard of beauty had diminished.

It hadn't.

As Gordon walked around his car after dropping off his keys with the valet, he took in the throng gathered in front of the club. The line of cars snaking around the joint made perfect viewing for all the onlookers. They didn't know what they were in for.

Another valet opened the passenger door. Gordon, carrying the camera bag over his shoulder, was there to offer his arm to Lucy Barnes.

Her black patent leather shoes were tall enough to elevate her a couple of inches. She stood and smiled for the cameras, deftly adjusting her black evening dress along the curves of her body. Her necklace matched her dangling earrings. Her brunette hair was swept up and over her shoulder, held in place by a barrette that matched the earrings and necklace. Her radiant smile was framed by red lips.

Involuntarily, Gordon's stomach flipped twice. She was beautiful. He wasn't the only one who thought so. Photographers stationed outside the doors snapped pictures, the flashes illuminating the already bright night. One celebrity reporter who recognized him shouted, "Gordon, who's the gal?"

Now Gordon was there for a job and only a job. Even his connections might not have been enough to score him a ticket if he weren't attending as part of the press. It was rare that he was on this side of news. Every man has a natural tendency to brag when he has a beautiful woman on his arm. Gordon stifled that urge and merely stated, "This is Lucy Barnes of the *Post-Dispatch*. We're here to learn about Bruno Clavell. Read about it tomorrow."

Lucy wobbled a bit and held on tighter to Gordon's arm. Under her breath and through a smile, she murmured, "Let's get inside so people will stop watching us."

"I don't think people are going to stop watching you. Me? In a New York minute."

They slipped inside and presented their tickets, along with their press credentials. They were ushered to a side area where Gordon plopped down the camera bag.

Lucy sat on a chair and extended her legs. She groaned.

"It's one thing to be on the back side of a camera taking pictures of celebrities in clothes and shoes that look great but are hell on the body"—she used the toe of one shoe to ease the pressure on the heel of the other—"but it's another thing entirely to wear them."

"A girl like you isn't used to wearing clothes like that?"

"Oh, I can wear them. There are some benefits to working for *Vogue*. I just don't have a lot of opportunities to."

She stood and unpacked her camera equipment with an efficiency Gordon had seen only when soldiers broke down their weapons. In no time, she was ready.

"Thanks, by the way, for saying what you said out there. I've dated some men who just want to show off with me on their arm. It's kind of insulting, to be honest."

"Of course, my lady." Gordon made a courtly stage bow. Inside, he was glad to have averted a crisis. "What do you need for your part?"

"Various shots of Clavell doing what Bruno Clavell does so well: mingling with the rich and famous, being a famous nightclub owner, you know, things like that. Also, I'd like to meet him, size him up, perhaps even get him for a posed shot."

One side of Gordon's mouth turned upward. "Might I trouble you for a dance sometime this evening?"

She looked at him. "I'm new in town. How do I know if you're a gentleman?"

Gordon looked hurt. "Well, you'll just have to find out. Come on, let's get to work."

Before leaving Clavell's apartment that afternoon, Gordon had arranged for a few minutes with him during the festivities. Clavell's only caveat was that Gordon kept his notepad out of sight. Having reporters was a necessary item on Clavell's agenda, but they didn't have to look like reporters. Photographers, on the other hand, were encouraged to snap pictures and be seen doing so.

Levitz had told both of them to get themselves introduced to Clavell early on. "I want him to remember that the *Post* is the only paper in town to send a guy and a gal to this party." Gordon and Lucy meandered through the throng, Lucy keeping her camera by her side as discreetly as possible.

No one could wonder where Bruno Clavell stood. The small gaggle of people laughing, chatting, and angling to get closer was obvious from across the room. He stood near the bandstand radiant as the nucleus of the group. Benny Goodman walked over, clarinet in hand, and asked Clavell a question. The owner nodded and Goodman turned to his band. He counted off and "Sing Sing Sing" blasted out. The partygoers cheered and started to dance. The dance floor swarmed with people and Gordon and Lucy had trouble traversing.

"I almost want to start dancing," Gordon said. "It might be easier."

"Later." Lucy's eyes were fixed on Clavell. "Let me get my shots."

Smaller in stature than Gordon, she snaked through the throng to the other side of the dance floor and approached Clavell. He hadn't caught sight of her. Instead, he was gazing across his new establishment with the look of a man in complete control and in complete happiness.

The flash from Lucy's camera brought him out of his reverie. He turned and caught sight of her. She grinned, not showing teeth, and approached him, holding out her hand. "I'm Lucy Barnes, *Post-Dispatch*. It's a pleasure to meet you, Mr. Clavell."

He took her hand and shook it with both of his. "The pleasure is all mine, Miss Barnes. And please call me Bruno. All my friends do."

"Am I your friend?"

"I sincerely hope so." Catching sight of Gordon, Clavell said, "Mr. Gardner, I can see why you kept her from me this afternoon. The reveal is much more spectacular than it would have been earlier."

Gordon nodded once. "It's all part of the news business, Mr. Clavell. Everything seems to be going well so far. Any issues?"

"Not a one." Clavell released Lucy's hand. "Things are going splendidly."

Another woman approached them. "Ah, Mr. Gardner, have you met Mrs. Myrna Loy?"

Gordon turned and gazed at the beauty that was Myrna Loy. Trying to hide the fact he was star-struck, he extended his hand. *Please don't let me stammer.* "Mrs. Loy, it's a pleasure to meet you."

Clavell said, "Don't believe everything he says, Myrna. Mr. Gardner here is a reporter."

The actress chuckled and took Gordon's hand. "Pleased to meet you. And you as well." She shook Lucy's hand. "And you are?"

"Dancing with me." Clavell took Lucy's camera and gave it to Gordon. "Hold this, Mr. Gardner." Taking Lucy by the hand, he led her to the dance floor. "Sing Sing

Sing" had finished. Now the band was playing "Stompin'
at the Savoy."

Myrna Loy tapped Gordon on the sleeve. "That's the
kind of thing that only happens in movies."

He put the camera down on the stage. "So is regular
joes getting to dance with beautiful actresses." He
gestured to the floor. "May I have this dance?"

She nodded. The two of them joined the dancers.
They made small talk, mostly about her roles in movies,
especially the three "Thin Man" movies that Gordon
loved so much. She asked him about his work and he let
on that he was a pulp writer on the side.

It was during the final minute of the song that Gordon
spotted a face he was looking for. The same face that had
looked out of the doctor's office window that afternoon.
Dr. Kermit Kernow. The doctor stood near the bar sipping
champagne.

"Mr. Gardner," Myrna Loy said, shifting her face so
that she could get Gordon's attention, "have you found
something more exciting than a Hollywood star?"

"There's a man I have to see." Gordon excused
himself. A flash bulb went off but Gordon hardly noticed.

Kernow wore a fitted black suit with a red tie. The
gray along his temples gave him a distinguished look.
The lights of the hall reflected off his round spectacles.
Depending on the angle, you couldn't even see his eyes.
He chatted with a few other men as they looked at the
gala.

"Dr. Kernow?" Gordon extended his hand.

The doctor's countenance changed. He shook the proffered hand stiffly. "Yes?"

"I'm Gordon Gardner of the *Post-Dispatch*."

"I know who you are, Mr. Gardner. You came by my office this afternoon." The gentlemen next to Kernow began to pay closer attention.

"I was wondering if you could comment on the types of medications you were prescribing a client?"

Kernow smiled thinly. "You know I cannot do that."

"Yes, but the patient is dead. Doesn't that render whatever contract you had null and void?"

"Actually, no," said one of the men in the group. "That contract extends past death." He put out his hand. "Harry Haldeman, attorney at law."

Undeterred, Gordon shook the hand. "What about during criminal investigations? Is there an exception?"

"What crime has been committed?" Haldeman asked.

"The death of one of his patients. Victor Tompkins."

"Mr. Tompkins died a tragic death, but hardly a criminal one." Kernow finished his champagne in one last gulp. "This is a party, Mr. Gardner. Why not try to have a little fun and leave off the snooping to another time? I'd hate to have my friend here contact your paper and report your harassment."

CHAPTER NINE

Gordon walked into Levitz's office the next morning and closed the door. "Who called?"

"Harry Haldeman," Levitz replied. "On behalf of his friend, Dr. Kernow."

"Who took the call?"

"Our ombudsman, John. You're familiar with him, I think?"

"Very much so. He's usually wrong on many things."

"But he's not wrong on this. You stepped out of line. You messed up with Clavell. You messed up Lucy's material."

"How?"

"By calling attention to yourself and this little thorn in your side."

"Boss, you know my thorns are good, right?"

"Not this time," Levitz huffed. "Besides, you left Myrna Loy alone on the dance floor. We have the photo to prove it. You've seen the photo, right? The one with you walking away and Mrs. Loy looking stunned."

Gordon had seen it, in the *Houston Tribune*, the local tabloid. "Eli, there's a reason Kernow is shutting this down. He's dirty. He has something to do with this. Give me a few more days and I can..."

"No. I stood up for you with Mr. Preston but that

probably cost me. They wanted you sidelined for a week. I told them you were the only one who could write the Clavell piece. So, go home, write the piece, and take the rest of the week off."

Gordon sat in his chair open-mouthed. "Are you serious?"

"Absolutely. And they want you on a short leash when you get back." Levitz softened his face. "Look, Gordon, this'll blow over and then you can get back to it. But, for now, lie low."

Gordon didn't need to look out the office's windows. He pretty much knew all pairs of eyes were watching him. So be it.

He stood and straightened his tie. "Make sure no one gets my desk, especially Johnny."

"Sure."

Gordon opened the door and walked out of the office. Most people did their best to look away. Johnny Flynn's eye followed Gordon out of the room, smirking the entire time.

Outside the offices, Gordon blinked in the bright Houston sunlight.

"Hey, wait up!" Lucy Barnes hurried up to him, her camera bag slung over her shoulder. "Tough break, Gordon. Sorry about that."

"Thanks. I hope I didn't embarrass you last night."

"Not at all. While you got to dance with Mrs. Thin Man—before you ditched her—I got to dance with Mr. Thin Man, William Powell, and meet the mayor. Plus I got some good shots. I'm getting the prints developed in the dark room. And what are you going to do?"

He shrugged. "I have to write the Clavell piece."

"How long will that take?"

"Maybe half a day."

She angled her head. "How long will it really take?"

He cracked a grin. "Probably three hours. Why?"

She gave him a questioning look. "What's the scoop on that other thing you were so passionate about?"

"The Tompkins story? It was printed in the crime beat this morning. Officially, it's done."

"You satisfied with that?"

"Nope."

"You going to do anything about it?"

"I'm thinking about it."

"C'mon, buy me a cup of coffee and tell me what we're going to do next."

He frowned. "We?"

"Sure. I have a few hours before all the prints are ready for review. Then I have to wait on your story. Let's have a business meeting to discuss how the Clavell piece is going to go. In the meantime, tell me about your other story."

Gordon shoved his hands in his pockets. "Aren't you worried you might get stained by my reckless nature?"

"I take pictures of celebrities and famous people. That

can get boring. Maybe it's time for a change."

Gordon grunted. "It's your funeral."

He led her to his car and they drove to a nearby Shipley Do-Nut shop. Over coffee and doughnuts, he related what he had learned about Tompkins—not much—his suspicions about Kernow—not much—and his ideas on how they were related.

"So you don't have much?" Lucy said.

"Nothing more than a hunch."

"How far do your hunches usually go?"

"To the front page."

She pursed her lips. "What do you want? The front page or the truth?"

He sat a moment thinking.

"Let me put it another way: are you still thinking about it because you want the story or are you wanting to uncover some secret?"

Gordon arranged the napkin and coffee cup in a precise order and used his finger to collect the crumbs. "With Victor Tompkins dead, Naomi and her husband now have to figure out what to do with their elderly mother. That was Victor's job. Now, whether it was merely an accident or an accident that could have been prevented, I aim to find out. Victor Tompkins clearly experienced something that made him think the cars were phantoms and I think it has something to do with the medicine he was taking. Why else would an otherwise normal man start thinking that kind of thing? So, that's what I'm gonna do. And I don't care if it gets me in hot water with

Levitz. It's the right thing to do."

Lucy Barnes stood. "That's my kind of righteousness. What's our next move, Ace?"

CHAPTER TEN

The Great Southern Encyclopedia Company was located in a cinder-block building down on the east side of town, a mile or so from the Houston Ship Channel. The company name and logo were painted on one side of the building and, on the other, an image of all sorts of things coming out of an open book.

"Guess that's supposed to be a sales point," Gordon said.

"Hang on, let me snap a picture." Lucy pulled out her camera and captured the image.

"What's all the fuss about this?" Gordon asked.

She looked at him, hair cascading around her shoulders. "I told you that you have my kind of righteousness. When we find the truth, we'll need to lay it out to Levitz. It'll help to have pictures."

Gordon arched his eyebrow. "It's a good thing you weren't around a month ago. The story I uncovered with the help of my private investigator friend would've landed you in hot water."

"I'm intrigued."

"And you'll stay that way." He ran his thumb and forefinger across his lips. "Sworn to secrecy."

She pouted. "Then don't bring it up."

The interior of the building consisted of white walls with additional paintings extolling the virtue of owning and reading encyclopedias. A couple of salesmen sat at desks with phones to their ears.

A young woman approached the two reporters.

"We'd like to talk with the manager," Gordon said.

"What is this about?" the woman asked. She spoke to Gordon but kept looking at Lucy.

"Victor Tompkins," Gordon replied.

Her face drooped. "Oh. I see. Excuse me." She walked to the back of the office.

"Why didn't you tell her right off you were the press?" Lucy asked.

"Sometimes it's best to withhold that kind of information until you get to the person you want to see. That way, their natural reaction shows through."

One of the salesmen hung up the phone and strolled over to them. "Did I hear you asking about Victor?"

"Yes," Gordon said, "you knew him?"

"We shared the same circuit. Hal Andrews." He extended his hand, Gordon shook it, introducing himself and Lucy.

"What can you tell me about Victor?" Gordon asked.

"Not much, really. Good worker, great salesman. He could convince a guy who already had a set of encyclopedias that he needed another. Shame about what happened."

Lucy asked, "What did you think about how he acted this past month?"

Hal shrugged. "I didn't know much about that, really. The boss just told me I had to pick up some slack. I worked longer hours, but the paychecks were bigger, so that's not a bad thing, huh?" He grinned. "The boss'll tell you more." He leaned in and lowered his voice. "Is all that true, about what he said about those cars?"

"What did you hear him say?" Gordon asked.

Hal furrowed his brow. "That they were phantoms and disappeared into thin air."

"Did you happen to know what kind of medicine he was taking?"

Hal shook his head. "But I saw him taking pills frequently."

Another man walked up and introduced himself. "Alan McLean. I'm the manager of this branch. You were asking about Victor? In what context?"

"I'm Gordon Gardner. This is Lucy Barnes. We're from the *Post-Dispatch*. We're looking into Mr. Tompkins's death."

Alan had a puzzled look on his face. "Why?"

Gordon's eyebrows rose. "Because of the odd circumstances surrounding his death."

Alan nodded. "His death was odd, as you say, but what do you hope to gain by publishing the story?"

"We have reason to believe," Lucy said, "that Mr. Tompkins might've been under the influence of some sort of medication and were wondering if you knew what he was taking and why."

Alan's eyes took in his immediate surroundings. "Hal,

do you know?"

"No, sir. Victor never told me."

"He didn't tell me either. But it started to affect his work. Victor was a fantastic salesman. Could sell anything to anyone. But then about a month ago, he just up and stopped."

"Stopped?" Gordon asked. "Working?"

"Yeah. He took a sick day and then another. Then he would just miss days." Alan winced. "We talked about it and he promised to get back on track. But it didn't happen." He scratched the back of his neck. "I had to let him go."

Gordon and Lucy exchanged glances. "That's interesting," Gordon said. "When we talked with his family, we didn't get any indication that he'd stopped working."

"Perhaps he didn't tell them."

"Maybe not, but his mom and sister were under the impression he was working until the day he died."

Alan shrugged. "I don't know what to tell you. He wasn't working here."

"Could you tell us what that last route was that Victor had?"

"Sure." Alan walked back to his office.

"What are you thinking?" Lucy said.

"Not sure. A hunch. A wish. Maybe the thing that caused all of Victor's problems is on that last route. Let's see where it is."

Alan returned and handed Gordon a slip of paper with directions. "It's out east of here. Country roads and tall pine trees. We've not had much success so I sent Victor out there hoping he could crack it. He never did."

"And there was nothing unusual about this last route?" Gordon asked.

"Not really." Alan chuckled. "Oh, well there was the one thing, yeah. He got run off by an old geezer with a rifle."

CHAPTER ELEVEN

The farmhouse sat at the end of a small dirt road. Tall pine trees obscured the road from the paved road so much so that Gordon missed the turn and had to double back.

He eased his Lincoln Zephyr up the road, gravel and dirt crunching under the tires. The smell of pine, manure, and turned earth filled the air.

"Better leave your camera bag here. You don't want Mr. Miller thinking anything looks suspicious."

"Agreed," Lucy said. "This whole area is light on people. When was the last house?"

"A mile or so back. Who knows how far until the next one? I can see why the encyclopedia company had a hard time making inroads." He nodded to the house. "We've been spotted. Let's go."

They climbed out of the car and walked up to the front yard. The woman of the house wore a dirty dress. She wiped her hands on a towel slung over her shoulder. A young boy clung by her side.

"My husband's on the way here," she said. "What y'all want?"

Gordon tipped his hat to her. "Hello, ma'am. My name's Gordon Gardner. This is Lucy Barnes. We work for the *Post-Dispatch*. We were wondering if you could help us out."

The woman squinted. "With what?"

"We're looking to find out what happened to Victor Tompkins."

"Who?"

"Victor Tompkins, the traveling salesman who sold encyclopedias."

A funny smirk crossed her face. "Oh, him. We run him off our property. He was trespassin'. Like y'all are. We can't help you."

Lucy glanced at the little boy. "We?"

"Me and my husband." The woman pointed behind them.

Gordon and Lucy turned to see a man standing there. He wore beat-up overalls, and work boots. He held a pitchfork in his hand. Over his shoulder, a rifle hung on a strap.

"What do y'all want with us?" the man asked.

"Mr. Miller," Gordon began, "we're just wondering if y'all could help us. We're trying to find out what happened to Victor Tompkins, the traveling salesman who came here about a month ago."

"Don't know, don't care," Miller said. "I run that sonuvabitch off our property." When he talked, his mouth barely moved. "I knowed he was trouble the second I laid eyes on him. He was all dressed nice like the rest of'em. He started talking and we stopped listening."

Gordon held up a finger. "What do you mean by 'the rest of them'?"

"Folks in fancy clothes. Kinda like y'all. Besides, I was proved right. He got hisself in a heap of trouble after he left here."

Lucy asked, "What do you mean?"

"Who y'all with?"

"The *Post-Dispatch*," Gordon said.

"This for a story in the paper?"

"Yes."

"Then I ain't talking. Now git off my land. I don't want no trouble."

Gordon spread his palms out and up in what he hoped was a placating gesture. "What if we didn't even mention you? All we're asking from you is to help us understand what happened. Besides, Mr. Tompkins has died."

"Died?" Mrs. Miller said.

"Yes, ma'am," Gordon said. "He was hit by a car."

"He died from that?" Mr. Miller said. "I thought old man Hastings helped him."

Gordon held up a finger. "Who is old man Hastings?"

"Fella who lives down the road a bit. He's the one who saw the salesman hurt on the side of the road. Damned other car never stopped to help, from what I heard."

Gordon reached into his jacket to get his notebook.

Mr. Miller moved the pitchfork to a defensive position.

"It's just my notebook, sir. You're telling me things I've not heard before. I'd like to write them down. I won't use your name." He pulled out his notebook and showed it to Miller. The old farmer squinted his eyes, then relaxed.

"You want to go inside the house?" Gordon asked.

"Nope."

"Fine, then, we'll talk here. Now what's this about a car hitting Mr. Tompkins?"

"Don't know the whole story. He left here and didn't come back. Best I can figure, he had car trouble and walked to the nearest station up yonder."

"Which direction is yonder?"

"North. Don't get smart with me."

"I'm not. Go on."

Miller cleared his throat and spat. "This here salesman was a measly type anyway. He was looking all around our house with wild eyes. When I scared him off, he knew enough not to come back here. You follering me?"

"Crystal clear. So Mr. Tompkins had car trouble. He was walking on the road?"

"Yeah. Old man Hastings come over a rise and saw this big car swerve and hit a man. Turned out this man was the salesman. The other car turned around and Hastings thought they were gonna help. He slowed down to help, too, when he saw the other car try to run down the salesman. The other'n must've seen Hastings because it drove off real fast."

A moment of silence ensued while Gordon wrote furiously. Lucy filled the void. "Are you telling me Mr. Hastings saw someone try to run Tompkins down?"

"That's exactly what he said he saw."

Gordon and Lucy exchanged glances. "That might

explain why he was so paranoid about cars chasing him," Lucy said.

"Yes, but not why he thought they were phantom automobiles." Gordon turned to the farmer. "Where does Mr. Hastings live?" He copied down what Miller said.

"You can always talk to the sheriff," Miller said. "There might've been a report, lot of good it've done."

"Why do you say that?" Gordon asked.

Miller shrugged. "Sheriff ain't doin' a lotta of good 'round here. More of a nuisance, if you ask me."

Gordon thought a moment. "This is Montgomery County, isn't it? That means we're under the jurisdiction of James Roscoe."

"That's him," Miller said. "Now, about your paper. Why's a reporter from Houston out here asking about all this?"

Gordon closed his notebook and slipped it back into his pocket. "Because Mr. Tompkins was run down by a car in Houston three days ago. He claimed the car was a phantom and jumped in front of it to prove himself right. He didn't."

"Why'd a man be fool enough to do that?" Miller's wife said.

"That's what we aim to find out," Gordon said.

CHAPTER TWELVE

An hour later, Gordon and Lucy stood along Highway 15 with Bob Hastings. The old man wore heavy khakis and a heavy work shirt sweat-stained under the armpits. A straw hat covered his head, but he still wiped the perspiration with a bandana. The smell of sawdust wafted with him.

"Okay, so you see," Hastings began, "I come over that rise yonder." He made a cutting motion with his hand. "When I did, I done saw the man, um, what did you say his name was?"

"Victor Tompkins," Gordon said. "He was a traveling salesman, sold encyclopedias. You have a set?"

"Naw," Hastings said. "An old woodworker like me don't have much use for encyclopedias."

"I suspect Mr. Tompkins might've given you a real good reason to buy a set. Anyway, what did you see?"

"Right, so I come over that rise and I saw the man running away from me, oh, about two hundred yards from my truck."

"And that's here?" Lucy walked over to the spot and looked back up the rise to the south.

"Yes, ma'am."

Tall pine trees nearly reached the road on both sides. A shallow ditch framed both sides of the two-lane highway. "Any idea where he was running from?"

"No, ma'am. So, this other car, a maroon number,

Oldsmobile I think, was chasing this man. The car swerved and clipped him. This Tompkins fella had tried to jump but didn't make it entirely. He fell into this shallow ditch. The car was going so fast it run in that ditch also, but ahead of the fella. I didn't hear anything on account of my winders were up. I thought it mighta been an accident, but then that car got back on the road and turned to the man."

"Back on the road?" Lucy listened to Hastings but kept her eyes focused on the ground. Her camera was in her hands and she was angling for a good shot.

"Yes, ma'am. It was swerving back on the road after it had slid down near the ditch. It hadn't rained so the ground was dry. The only thing I could think happened was that the car went in the ditch on purpose and the only purpose I could think of was to hit that man."

"Where was he?" Gordon asked.

"Here." Hastings walked over to an area. "He was here, hobbling towards me."

"Back in the direction he was running from when you saw him?"

"Yes, sir. He saw my car and started waving his hands."

Lucy walked to the spot and snapped a photo of the ground. Skid marks were still visible on the pavement.

"There's no way to prove those marks belonged to the maroon Olds," Gordon said to her.

"I know, but it helps me document the story with my pictures. You see, I tell stories with my camera. Even if the subjects are only celebrities, I'm still writing a narrative. You know a picture is worth a thousand words."

"Don't remind me," Gordon said. "Sometimes I think future newspapers will have more pictures than words and reporters like me will be out of a job. It's why I write other things on the side." To Hastings he said, "So what happened next?"

"Well, when I see a fella waving his arms, I'm the kinda guy who stops to see what's going on. I slowed my truck and seen the other car come full circle and drive back to the man. The driver musta seen me because he kept making a loop and drove off real fast in the other direction. It got outta here in a real hurry."

"So this other car just drove off," Gordon said. "Have you seen it again?"

"No, sir."

"And you'd never seen it ahead of time?"

"No, sir. The only other car on the road was way up yonder. It was pulled off to the side of the road. I found out that was the salesman's car. It had broken down and that's why he was walking."

"About where was the man's car?" Lucy asked.

"There next that pine tree that's leaning over."

Lucy chuckled. "There are pine trees everywhere. It's hard to see even twenty feet into the forest, it's so dense." She aimed her camera in the direction and snapped a photo.

"What happened to the salesman's car?" Gordon asked.

"Local tow company came and got it. A few days later when I went back in town, I ran into the tow truck driver. I asked him what happened to the car. He said there was a hole in the carburetor."

"A hole?" Gordon said.

"Yeah. I asked what kind of hole. He didn't know, but he coulda swore it was a bullet hole."

Lucy and Gordon looked at each other. Gordon asked Hastings the name of the tow truck driver.

Hastings gave the name but then said, "The salesman came and picked up his car a few days later. Had another tow truck from the city come and take it back."

Gordon wrote more in his notebook. Lucy started walking to the spot where Hastings said Tompkins's car had died.

"Okay, Mr. Hastings, you've been a great help. Do you mind if I quote you in the story?"

The old man's smile lit up his face. "I ain't been in the paper since I joined the army in 1917. I'd love to be in the paper. Which one again?"

"*Post-Dispatch*." To Lucy, he called, "you gonna walk the entire way?"

"Yes," she called from over her shoulder.

Gordon nodded to his car. "I think I'll pick her up down there. I have your number. Can I call you if I have any more questions?"

"Sure," Hastings said. The two men shook hands and Hastings climbed into his truck and drove away. Gordon got behind the wheel of his car and eased it into neutral.

The machine slowly moved down the hill, picking up speed. He stopped and parked when he came abreast of Lucy. She snapped another photo. "See anything interesting?"

"Not really."

He got out and walked beside her. "A bullet hole. But it couldn't have happened here. The forest is too dense. I've hunted deer around here and I'll be damned if it's easy."

"Mr. Miller could've shot the car to discourage Tompkins from coming back."

Gordon shook his head. "I got the sense Miller was just trying to protect himself. I don't think he'd have actually shot anyone."

Lucy stopped and looked all around. "There's nothing here but trees, this two-lane, and the sky. Tompkins's car breaks down. He surely isn't going to go back that way, to the Millers, after he received such a warm reception, right?"

"Right."

"So that means he must have been walking this way, to the north. But as far as I can see, it's at least a mile or so until you get to that next bend and who knows what's that way or how close the next house is. Not that you'd know it from the geography." She pointed back in the direction they had come. "Even that last private road we saw was barely visible. If it weren't for the mailbox at the roadside, I'd have missed it completely. I'm not sure how a bullet would've nailed the car but I'm guessing it was the reason why Tompkins was running."

Gordon inhaled deeply and let the air blow through his lips. He tipped his hat higher on his forehead and looked in all directions. "I know what you mean."

Lucy stood in place and snapped photos of the entire area, turning in place to capture all angles.

The sound of a car coming over the rise caught their ears. They turned and noticed a police car moving down the highway. It slowed and stopped behind Gordon's car. A man, tall and gangly, got out and hooked his thumbs in his belt. "You folks okay?"

Lucy gave Gordon a quick look but the reporter just put on one of his thousand-dollar grins. "We're fine, sir, just fine. Gordon Gardner, Lucy Barnes, we're from the *Houston Post-Dispatch*."

The deputy came closer to them and spat on the ground. His name tag caught the light and Gordon read, "Poole." "Y'all're a long way from the city. Why y'all out here?"

Gordon told him about following up on the accident on this stretch of the highway with Victor Tompkins. When asked if he remembered the incident, Poole chuckled. "Ain't much happens around here we don't know about. Sure, I remember. It wasn't me that arrived first. It was Nagel, but I heard all about it. The traveling salesman was trying to sell encyclopedias or something, got his car broke, and was walking for help when another car clipped him. Hurt his leg, but didn't break it. A local fella stopped to help but the other car had already skedaddled."

"Did y'all file a report?" Gordon asked.

Poole shrugged. "We were going to wait for the

injured man to get out of the hospital and come by but he never did. We don't usually file an official report unless the victim does it. We asked him about it as he's lying in bed at the hospital but all he ever said was that…" Poole paused and frowned.

"What?" Gordon said.

Poole scratched his chin. "It's weird, that salesman. It was like he wasn't all there, you know." He pointed to his head and twirled around his finger in the universal gesture that meant crazy. "He was talking so much gibberish that we just figured he got hit harder'n we thought. Musta messed with his head. We decided to let him sleep it off and ask him again later. We got his car towed. We come back the next day and he'd checked himself out."

"Was he able to walk?" Lucy said.

Poole shrugged. "Well enough or the doc wouldn't have let him go. He called someone in town, sister I think. She came and got him. He sent for his car later. Since he didn't file a report, we didn't think any more of it. Which brings me back to my question." He leveled his gaze at the two reporters. "Why are y'all up here?"

"Because someone ran that man down and killed him three days ago," Gordon said.

Poole raised his eyebrows. "Not sure how I see that relates to his little incident up here."

"We don't either," Gordon said, "and it may not. But we were just following up on his last route. We got word that he was saying some weird things just before he was killed. You said he was saying gibberish up here. Any chance you remember what he was saying?"

"Just what Nagel told me. He said the man was talking about cars vanishing into thin air." The guffaw that erupted from Poole was loud and boisterous. "You ever heard such a silly thing as that?"

"Actually," Gordon said, "we have. And now we've heard it twice."

CHAPTER THIRTEEN

"I think it's perfectly clear that Victor Tompkins saw something he wasn't supposed to see and that got him shot at." Lucy sat in the passenger seat of Gordon's car as they drove back to Houston.

They had spent the rest of the morning following up on interviews. First was the attending physician, a Dr. Stephen Dickson at the local Montgomery hospital. He confirmed that Tompkins had sprained his knee and ankle but, with some pain medication, was able to walk well enough with a cane to check himself out of the clinic and be picked up by his sister. The tow truck driver corroborated that he towed Tompkins's car back to his lot and then was paid to fix the carburetor. But that was over a month ago.

"You're right," Gordon said, "but what in blue blazes did he see? Better yet, why didn't Naomi Wilson mention this to us when we spoke to her?"

"You think she might be hiding something?"

"We're going to find out. We're going straight there now." He hit the steering wheel with his fist. "But I still can't figure out how Kernow fits into this."

Lucy shrugged. "Maybe the answer is still buried in something we haven't seen yet."

A small curl graced Gordon's lips. "I like the sound of that."

"What?"

"We."

She harumphed. "I'll admit this is a whole lot more fun than celebrities telling me which is their better side over and over again. You usually do this all by yourself?"

"Yup. Most reporters do. We get to be the lone wolf and uncover all the dirty little secrets hidden in this town." He grew silent for a moment.

Lucy picked up on his mood. "What are you thinking?"

He looked off in the other direction. "It's nothing. It's just that sometimes, the things you learn make you uneasy, like you don't know the real world until you uncover all the rocks. The problem is you don't always like what you see under them."

They stopped at a cafe on the outskirts of Houston and ate lunch. Afterwards, they made their way back to the house of the late Victor Tompkins.

"You told me he lived with his mom," Lucy said, "but you didn't tell me the house was as old as it is." She put up her fingers and thumbs and made a rectangle to mimic a camera lens. "This would be a neat house to shoot."

"Wait until you get a glimpse of the inside." He walked up and knocked on the door. A few moments later, a man answered. "You must be Gardner, the reporter. I'm Samuel Wilson, Naomi's husband." He opened the door and let both reporters into the house.

"Wow," Lucy said under her breath. "It's like slipping back in time."

"I had the same thought. Now, imagine you're Victor and living here."

Naomi and her mother were in the breakfast room having sandwiches and coffee. Gordon introduced Lucy.

Naomi busied herself with a couple more cups of coffee. They all took seats; Samuel next to Naomi with Gertrude at the head of the table, and Gordon began.

"Mrs. Wilson, we've been doing some digging. A few things don't add up. One, your brother was fired from his job a little over three weeks ago."

Naomi's mouth hung open. "Are you sure?"

"We talked with his boss. Victor's behavior had become so erratic—missing work, late to work—that the boss had to let him go. You didn't know?"

"Not at all. Sure, I knew he called in sick sometimes because he'd call and let me know I didn't have to check on Mom but that was it. He got up, took care of her, and left for work up until last Friday."

"The day before he died," Lucy said.

Gordon leaned on his knees. "So you have no idea what he might have been doing when he wasn't here?"

Naomi looked at her husband and then back to Gordon. "I don't. I thought he was working." She shook her head as if trying to clear it. "But that doesn't matter, really."

Gordon frowned. "I think it matters a lot. We're trying to find out what happened."

"I know what happened. My brother died. Not in the woods but here in the city. On the side of the curb. I don't care what happened last month. I want to know what happened four days ago when that bastard ran my brother down." She paused and bored her gaze into

Gordon. "Have you even talked to the driver?"

That revelation, the most obvious fact he had missed, slammed into Gordon's brain like a freight train. He tried to cover with throat clearing. "Naturally he's on our list to talk with."

Naomi kept staring at Gordon. "You didn't even think of it, did you?"

Gordon held up a finger. "Truthfully, no, because the theft of your brother's medication led me in a different direction. It made me think that was the angle. Now that we're at somewhat of an impasse, we will follow up with the driver. You obviously know about him. Where'd you hear it from?"

"The police, when they came to tell me about Victor. The other guy landed in the hospital. Not sure if he's still there."

Naomi paused and sipped her coffee. "Mr. Gardner, why are you doing this? Why write about Victor's death?"

Gordon sat up and tapped his notebook in his hands. "When I got assigned this story, I was told it was merely a crime beat story. But when I learned about the theft of his medicines and the shutout by his doctor, I got suspicious. I figured there's something more going on. And someone is behind it. Now that we know about Victor being shot at out in the woods, I'm even more convinced a light needs to shine in a dark hole. I am that light."

He wiped his brow with his fingertips and sipped his coffee.

"Despite my boyish charm, I've been around long enough to know that when people get killed, there's a bigger story behind it, a story that involves bad people. What I do is find the truth and shine the light. I am the lighthouse on the raging ocean of evil in this town. Your brother got himself caught up in something and I'm going to find out what it was and expose it and bring those responsible to justice."

"You're quite passionate, Mr. Gardner. I'll give you that. But how do you expect to do that when I hear you're off the story?"

Gordon's brow furrowed in confusion.

"I called the paper to leave you a message. I wanted to let you know I had spoken with the police about Peter Kingsbury. He's the man who killed my brother. Imagine my surprise when I was told you were not on the story, that there wasn't even a story to be written."

Gordon stood. "There is a story here, Mrs. Wilson. And I'm going to tell it. One way or another."

CHAPTER FOURTEEN

"Look," Gordon said, "I'm already in hot water. No need to swamp you, too. I'm taking you back to the newsroom." He aimed his Zephyr towards the *Post-Dispatch* building.

"There's time for that later," Lucy said. "Let's go see Kingsbury. You've set the book, Ace. I'm in it until the end."

Gordon gave her a skeptical look. "You sure? I don't wanna ruin your time here in town."

"You kidding? This is the most interesting thing I've ever shot."

"It's your funeral." Gordon executed a perfect u-turn and headed away from the newsroom.

"Besides, you get anywhere near the *Post* and someone sees you, you can't keep going. You build more evidence, then perhaps Mr. Levitz will let you write the story."

Gordon sighed. "You don't know Levitz. Besides, there are other ways to get the truth out there."

"Tabloids?"

"Yeah, that, but pulp fiction stories, too."

"You're joking."

"Not at all. You'd be surprised how many folks read those magazines and what kind of seed you can plant. It just takes too long."

"And how would you know that?" She half-turned in the seat.

He wagged his eyebrows. "Can I buy you dinner and tell you all about it?"

She smiled demurely. "I don't date colleagues."

"Too bad. It's one hell of a story." He parked his car at the hospital. "C'mon, let's go visit our killer driver."

Gordon stepped out of his car and spun around. "You see that?" He pointed down the street.

"What?" Lucy got out and came to stand next to him.

"A maroon car. Ever since hearing it was a maroon car, I've been seeing them everywhere. It's like when you grow a mustache and then you notice all the other men wearing them."

"I haven't had that experience, but I understand what you mean."

Gordon and Lucy checked in at the front desk of Houston Methodist Hospital, got directions, and climbed three flights to get to the room of Peter Kingsbury. Gordon knocked on the half-open door.

"Come in," said a man's voice.

The two reporters entered the room. What they found surprised them.

There was no patient in the bed. Instead there was a man, standing next to the window. He wore brown trousers with suspender straps draped around his waist but no shoes or socks. He was in the act of buttoning his shirt. Bandages covered his forehead and nose. His nose had a small brace running across it. The man's black hair was oily and disheveled.

"Peter Kingsbury?" Gordon said.

The man turned. "Yes?"

"I'm Gordon Gardner, this is Lucy Barnes. We're from the *Post-Dispatch* and we'd like to ask you a few questions about the accident."

Kingsbury's jaw muscles visibly tightened, causing him to wince in pain. "Like you said, it was an accident. Pure and simple."

"Be that as it may," Gordon said, "would you mind my asking you a few questions?"

"You're with the press?"

"Yes, sir."

"Why are you writing about the story?"

Gordon spread his hands. "We're looking into the death of the victim."

"The police cleared me, you know. They said the family wouldn't press charges." He finished buttoning his shirt and leveled a finger at Gordon. "Wait a minute. Y'all are working for them, right? Y'all are out to get me."

"No, sir," Lucy said. "We work for the paper and we're just trying to get some background on the victim. We've talked with numerous eyewitnesses and we'd like to get your side of the story, too."

"I don't have a side." Kingsbury sat on the bed and reached for his socks. He started forcefully pulling them on.

"Then could you tell us what happened from your point of view?" Gordon pulled out his notebook and readied his pencil.

Kingsbury shrugged. "What's to tell? I was driving along the street and this guy jumps in front of my car. I didn't have time to swerve although I tried. I'm a good driver. It's what I do for a living."

"Yeah?" Gordon said. "You a taxi driver?"

"No. I work for the bank, driving trucks. But that's not important. I'm telling you I tried to swerve but didn't have time. I couldn't go to the right on account of all the people standing at the bus stop. So I went left but there wasn't enough time." He paused, one sock half on, staring at the floor. "I hit that man," he said in a smaller voice, "and killed him."

Gordon cleared his throat. "It's a tragedy. And an accident. Did you happen to notice anything weird or out of the ordinary about the man before you hit him?"

Kingsbury finished putting on the sock and laced up his shoe. "It happened too fast. It was a blur."

"How fast were you going?"

"Not slow enough to stop." He put on his other sock.

"Did the police talk to you?"

"Sure. At the street just after it happened. I was messed up real bad." He gestured to his face. "They brought me here thinking I mighta messed up my head. It was strange, really. In all my years of driving, I ain't never hit nothing. It's the only thing I'm good at and you'd never expect hitting a man could do so much damage to a driver."

Gordon frowned and gave Lucy a quick look. "You hunt, Mr. Kingsbury?"

He looked up at Gordon, curious. "Yeah. Why?"

"Well, lots of folks who drive out to the country crash into deer crossing the road. It can cause lots of damage. Even kills some drivers. So don't be surprised at how bad you got messed up. Did the doctors clear you of a concussion?"

"Yeah, just today. It's why I'm leaving."

"Going home?"

Kingsbury shot Gordon a look. "Of course I'm going home. Where else would I go?"

"Nowhere." Gordon put his notebook into his jacket, then pulled it back out. "So, in our story, we'll have to list your details. Usually this includes your street name and place of work. I can get that kind of thing from the county courthouse or the police report, but can you just give me those details now?"

"Police report? I was told there wasn't a police report."

"C'mon, Mr. Kingsbury, there was an accident that resulted in a death. Of course there's a police report. Who told you there wasn't one? One of the detectives on the case?" Gordon flipped back through the pages mumbling various names.

"Wilson."

Gordon arched an eyebrow. "Like the president?"

"Sure." Kingsbury stood and took a tie off the back of

a chair. "That detective said there would be no report."

"Well, it might be a minor report but it'll at least be something." He snapped his fingers. "Lucy, did the mother say she was going to press charges? Or the sister?"

Lucy was somewhat flummoxed by Gordon's chatter. "I can't remember. They're pretty hard up. Not sure how they'll make it without Victor."

Kingsbury hurriedly knotted his tie, leaving it askew but not caring. "I have to go."

"Back home? I didn't get that street name."

"You'll have to look it up," Kingsbury pulled out a valise that looked brand-new and packed his accouterments.

"And your place of employment. You said you worked for a bank, driving trucks. Which bank?"

"Um, Amherst National."

"Thank you. Say, that's a fine looking case you got there. It must have cost a pretty penny. Where'd you get it? Harold's in the Heights?"

"Not sure. It was a gift." Kingsbury zipped the case closed and looked for his coat.

"Heck, I want your friends." Gordon chuckled. "Your jacket's over here on the door hook." He handed the tan suit coat to Kingsbury.

"Thanks. Are you really going to put this in the paper?"

"It depends on the editor. But it's looking like it's a

go, at least for the crime beat."

Kingsbury wagged his finger. "I knew it. I knew it." He walked over to the side table and grabbed a folded newspaper and shook it. "You've already written something. It's in today's paper!"

Without missing a beat, Gordon said, "Of course. That's the initial story. But there's something more."

"How do you know that?" Kingsbury demanded.

Gordon tapped his nose. "I've got a nose for news."

"Well, it's got nothing to do with me. All I was doing was driving. And that guy jumped in front of my car. I couldn't swerve in time and I hit him. I'm absolutely sick about it but I have to move on. Now, if you'll excuse me, I have to get home." He brushed past Gordon and Lucy on his way out of the room.

Gordon checked his watch.

"What's that for?"

"He gets a ten-second head start, then we follow him. How fast can you go down the stairs with those heels?"

She clicked them on the floor. "They're thick. No problem."

"Good. Let's go."

Gordon eased his head out of the room then stepped out to the nurses' station. "Mr. Kingsbury, which stairwell did he take?"

Over the top of her reading glasses, an old nurse said, "South."

Gordon and Lucy raced down the north stairwell,

Gordon taking them two at a time. He reached the lobby and eyed the people. Lucy came up behind him. "Glad I didn't bring my camera with me. Why are we doing this?"

"Something isn't right with him." Gordon glanced over his shoulder. "I wanna see where he goes."

"Why does that matter?"

"Not sure, but I'll tell you when I see it. Okay, got him. He's leaving."

Lucy tapped his shoulder. "Ace, think a minute. He couldn't have driven here. He probably came in an ambulance. So I doubt he's going to drive away."

"Right, I knew that. Still, let's see how he leaves."

They raced across the lobby and exited the building. On the street level, Kingsbury walked toward the front of the hospital. He stood, looking both directions. Gordon and Lucy had to duck behind a pillar to avoid being seen.

After a minute, a car pulled up beside Kingsbury. He looked around again and then got in the passenger seat. The car pulled away and merged into traffic.

"How good are your eyes? Did you get the tag?" Gordon pulled out his notebook and, after comparing what they saw, wrote down the license plate numbers. "Bob Hastings mentioned he thought the car that ran down Tompkins was a maroon Oldsmobile. That car was an Oldsmobile. And you saw the color, didn't you?"

Lucy nodded. "Maroon."

CHAPTER FIFTEEN

After a quick trip to the county courthouse where Gordon called in a favor from a clerk, they had both Peter Kingsbury's home address and place of employment. Deciding to see what kind of employee Kingsbury was, they headed over to the Lone Star Armored Truck Company off Waugh Drive. The building, in keeping with the type of work the firm conducted, was a squat two-story red brick structure with a wrought-iron fence around the entire perimeter.

A man in a guard booth opened and closed the gates. Gordon told the guard the reason for the visit. In a few minutes they were standing in the office of Martin Page. The man carried himself as former military with short-cropped hair, an impeccable suit, and excellent posture.

"What can I do for y'all?" Page's voice was a low baritone.

After Gordon made the introductions, he said, "We're working on a follow-up to the accident involving one of your employees, a Peter Kingsbury."

Like a steel cage, hardness descended over Page's face. "Peter's killing that man has no bearing on my company. Besides, he was an excellent driver."

"Mr. Page, this has nothing to do with your company. I'm just wondering what kind of man Mr. Kingsbury is. You say he's an excellent driver?"

"One of our best."

"Do your drivers have to pass specialized driving tests?"

"Yes."

"Does part of that exam include avoiding objects in the road?"

"What kind of driver's test would it be if it didn't?"

"And Mr. Kingsbury passed?"

"Of course. He had to in order to drive for me. Why all these questions about Peter?"

"Just getting a sense of him. Did he have a particular route?"

"All our drivers have a standard route and then get assigned a rotating list of additional ones. Peter usually covered north-central."

Gordon looked up to the ceiling, thinking. "North central. That's what, downtown up to North Main and over to Hardy?"

"Pretty much."

"All the banks in that section?"

"Yes."

"How was Mr. Kingsbury acting recently?" Lucy asked.

Page shifted his feet and slid his hands in his pockets. "We have a stressful job. We haul loads of cash and currency around. There's a lot of bad folks who would like to lighten our load. Our drivers like to blow off steam. Sometimes they may take it a little too far, but all men are like that, right?"

Gordon chuckled. "As rain."

"Peter's that way. I don't get much into my employees' lives as long as they do their jobs. Wait a minute." He put his fingers in his mouth and whistled. Heads turned. "Don, c'mere."

A man of about Gordon's age trotted over. "Yes, sir?"

"Anything strange going on with Peter, other than the accident?"

Don sucked air between his teeth. "Nothing more than usual. He's a little free with his money but hey, it's his money. He got all bent out of shape a couple months ago. Said he needed some cash. Was gonna work an extra job or something. Away from here."

Page turned to Gordon with raised eyebrows. "That all you need?"

Gordon closed his notebook. "Think so. When do you expect Mr. Kingsbury to return to work?"

"Next week."

Gordon thanked Page as he and Lucy walked out.

Out of earshot, Lucy said, "What was all that about Kingsbury's driving ability?"

"I just want a sense of him as a driver. Think about it: a man like Mr. Kingsbury is an excellent driver. He has to be to pass that driving test. Part of that test includes avoiding things in the road. When you swerve, you're likely to leave rubber on the road. But at the accident site, there were no swerve marks."

"Are you sure?"

"When I went to the intersection yesterday, I sketched the scene. I didn't notice any skid marks."

"What about blood?"

"Nothing either. Maybe someone hosed it away."

"Wouldn't the same apply for the rubber?"

"Not necessarily. Skid marks from car tires usually come from pieces of the rubber breaking off and melting into the cement. Much harder to wash away."

They both got in the car. "What do you think it means?"

Gordon started the car. He turned the wheel and headed back toward downtown. "Not only were there no swerve marks, but I didn't see any of the darker marks that usually mean someone slammed on the brakes."

Lucy slowly turned her head to Gordon, her mouth open in surprise. "You don't mean what I think you mean, do you?"

Gordon tightened his jaw, his muscles flexing. "The only reason I can see for no skid marks on the road is that Kingsbury never tried to stop his car. I think he hit Victor on purpose. To kill him."

CHAPTER SIXTEEN

Gordon pointed at the activity of the police station. "This is where you can spend a lot of time if you do criminal work." They sat in the lobby, waiting for Burt Wheeler to come into the lobby. He waved to Mike, the desk sergeant. Armed with his new theory, Gordon wanted to head over to the Amherst Bank and talk with the manager about Kingsbury's most recent activities, but Lucy insisted they come to the station. "This is getting bigger than a simple hit-and-run," she had said. "You're talking murder."

Gordon acquiesced although he didn't think it would amount to much.

"Gardner, how in the hell do you have such a pretty lady at your side?" Burt Wheeler strolled over to the bench and plopped himself down. He reached across Gordon and shook Lucy's hand as she introduced herself. "What brings you to hang around this clown?"

"Research," Lucy said, "and experience. Gordon is quite passionate when he gets around to it."

"Passion can only take you so far," Wheeler said. "After a while, you need evidence." He turned to Gordon. "So, what is it?"

Gordon withdrew his notebook. "Burt, I want you to hear me out before you start interrupting."

Wheeler scowled. "Interrupting's what I do, especially if the theory is cockamamie."

"Then I'll talk faster. So, you remember that guy, Victor Tompkins, who got hit by the car? Well, we've been doing some more research and…"

"Stop right there," Wheeler said. "The case is closed. End of story."

"I know," Gordon said, "but you might need to reopen it."

"No can do. The captain doesn't like to reopen closed cases. Did I mention it was closed?"

Gordon nodded and talked very evenly. "Yes, but just listen. Can you do that? Listen?"

Wheeler narrowed his eyes.

"Want Lucy to say it? Then it won't be coming from my mouth. Plus, she looks better than me."

The eyes narrowed more.

"Okay, Lucy, you start."

Surprised to be put on the spot, Lucy cleared her throat and spoke. "We started looking into Tompkins's actions leading up to his death. His mother and sister thought he was working up until last Friday. We talked to his boss and found out Tompkins was fired four weeks ago."

"So?

"So we talked to his boss and got Tompkins's last route. It's out east of here. What's the county?"

"Montgomery," Gordon said.

"Tompkins visits Montgomery County and something odd happens," Lucy continued.

"Don't care," Wheeler said. "As soon as you said Montgomery County, I stopped listening or caring. Out of our jurisdiction."

"Even if the weird thing was someone shooting at Tompkins's car or trying to run him down on the side of a road?" Lucy asked. Her voice had gotten stronger the more she talked.

"Where was he hit?" Wheeler said.

Lucy opened her mouth, paused, then said, "Here in Houston."

"Bingo," Wheeler said. "Houston. I'm a Houston police detective. I investigate crimes in Houston. I don't care what happens in Montgomery County." He put his hands on his knees and made to stand.

"What if I told you the person behind the wheel was an armored car driver who had an excellent record?" Lucy continued.

"Even the best drivers have accidents," Wheeler said. "The driver, um, what's his name?"

"Kingsbury," Gordon murmured.

"Yeah, in his statement, he said he sneezed and closed his eyes for a second or two. Boom. He hits the victim. It was an accident, pure and simple. The DA might press charges, but I doubt it. He's too swamped. The family of the victim hasn't come forward to press charges, so end of story."

Burt stood. "Besides, what were you planning on doing with this? Your paper already ran the crime beat story this morning. I'm pretty sure your editor won't want to run a correction." He patted Gordon on the shoulder. "Nice try, though. Next time, have more evidence." He strolled out of the lobby and back into the bowels of police headquarters.

Lucy patted Gordon's arm. "I'm sorry, Ace. Guess we're done."

Gordon stood. "Like hell, we're done. There's something there. You know it and I know it. C'mon, we're going to get more evidence."

"Where?"

"Amherst National Bank."

CHAPTER SEVENTEEN

The lobby of Amherst National Bank was large and spacious. The marble walls gleamed with the late afternoon sun. One featured a large, painted mural of various Texas landmarks and landscapes: the Alamo, bluebonnets, a basic Hill Country scene, the San Jacinto Monument, Sam Houston, Stephen F. Austin, and more. The painting flowed nicely with the Art Deco interior.

Gordon and Lucy asked for the bank manager. Within a few moments, Carl Bradshaw walked up to them, puzzled. "I thought you were working with Gerald."

"Um, no," Gordon said. "We're here to ask you a few questions about one of the armored truck drivers who had this route. Peter Kingsbury."

"Yes, I know Peter. Good man. Is this about that terrible accident I read about in the paper?"

"It is."

"Is there something more?"

"How was Mr. Kingsbury as a driver?"

"Fine. Just as good as every other driver who works for Mr. Page."

"When was the last time Mr. Kingsbury drove a route for you?"

Bradshaw thought a moment. "Last week. Our deliveries always go on Tuesdays. He was in the hospital today when we had our regularly scheduled appointment."

Lucy said, "Who showed in his place?"

"Well, Sammy, the guard, still came but there was a different driver. Mr. Page phoned ahead and told me of the switch."

"Is that standard?" Lucy asked.

"Every time."

"Any issues today?"

"None."

"What was the new guy's name?"

"Herbert."

"How was Mr. Kingsbury acting the last time you saw him?" Gordon asked.

"He was the same. Maybe a little distracted. You'll have to excuse me but I don't see what this has to do with me."

Another voice spoke up. "That's because Mr. Gardner is tilting at windmills again."

Gordon recognized the voice and whirled.

Johnny Flynn stood next to another man who wore a bronze name tag with "Gerald" engraved on it.

"Hello, Gordon. What rabbit trail led you here?"

Gordon narrowed his eyes. "I could ask you the same thing."

"You could, but then I'm working on a legitimate story. You know, the one I was assigned."

Gordon thought back and remembered the assignment. "The artist?"

In a sweep of his hand, Johnny indicated the mural. "William Silber's last masterpiece. Lucy, doll, you want to snap a photo of it for me? It'll look great next to my name on page one of the style section."

Lucy's jaw muscles tightened. She offered no response.

"You might take some free advice and get back to the newsroom and let this guy go. Gordie's already on thin ice. Now, that ice is cracking. I'd hate to see you get all wet."

"What are you talking about?" Gordon asked.

"Well, naturally you wouldn't know since you've been sneaking around. Imagine Levitz's surprise when he got a call from the sheriff of Montgomery County wondering why he had a reporter snooping around up there."

Gordon frowned.

"Naturally he denied that he had a reporter in Montgomery County because, well, he never assigned that story. Then he asked the sheriff who was out there. Gordon Gardner was the answer." Johnny paused and put a finger to his lips. "How loud do you think Levitz can yell?"

"I've heard him," Gordon muttered. "I've even heard him yell my name."

"Well, you missed it today. I didn't. I had a front row seat." He flicked his fingernails along his lapels. "Think he may have even spit on me."

"Excuse me, gentlemen," Bradshaw said, "but what has this to do with me and my bank?"

Johnny turned to the manager. "Absolutely nothing, sir. It's just an inconvenience for you. My apologies."

"Actually," Gordon said, "I've got some more questions for Mr. Bradshaw."

"That he doesn't have to answer because your little story won't ever see the light of day," Johnny retorted. "Face it, Gordon: this will likely be your last straw. Of all the shenanigans you've pulled in the past, this is by far the most egregious. The only thing left for you to do is clean out your desk." He inhaled and looked off into the middle distance. "I'm gonna love that desk."

Bradshaw motioned to Gerald. "Did you provide everything they need for the Silber piece?"

"Yes, sir."

"Then let's get back to work and let those two sort everything out themselves." Both bank employees walked back to their jobs.

Johnny's grin widened in triumph. "Real journalism, Gordon, is doing the jobs you're assigned."

"Real journalism," Gordon muttered, a snarl curling his lip, "is finding the truth when no one else is looking."

Johnny merely grunted. "Sure, but look where it's gotten you." He turned to Lucy. "I'd be happy to give you a lift and put in a good word on your behalf."

Lucy looked at both men. "I don't need anyone to stand up for me. But I do need to get these pictures developed.

To see what's what." She patted her case and winked at Gordon. "Sorry, Ace. I'll call you if I find anything." She patted his arm. "Okay, let's go."

Gordon Gardner stood alone. He watched Johnny hold the door open for Lucy and walk out. The afternoon sun was low on the horizon and the deep orange blazed into the lobby. Thoughts swirled in his head. He was certain that if he found the answer, Levitz would acquiesce and run his story.

But what was his story? What was the common thread? And even if he knew what it was, where was the proof?

Dejected, he walked to the door of the lobby. He glanced up at the painting again, then stopped.

"There's something here," he said. "But I'm not seeing it."

Another idea clicked into place. Smiling, Gordon walked a little faster.

CHAPTER EIGHTEEN

Gordon drove to the office of his friend, Benjamin Wade, private investigator, rather than to Wade's house. He was in luck; the office lights were on. Wade's grin was big and wide.

"Gordon Gardner, what brings you to my door?" He let the reporter into his office.

The desk in the waiting room was empty save for a typewriter, a desk blotter, and a bin of paper. The smell of typewriter ink and oil filled the room.

"Typing your own reports still?" Gordon asked.

"Yup, and will until I can find a secretary. You know how embarrassing it is to be a private eye without a secretary?"

"If you want one with looks, the gal I've been working with fits that bill."

"She the one with you last night?" Wade asked. "Saw your picture in the paper. Not very flattering."

"Thanks. What are you working on?"

"Still putting the final touches on the Rosenblatt case. I've got an appointment with a man named Elmer Weeks tomorrow or the next day." He fumbled through his desk calendar, flipping pages. "No, three days from now. Who knows what that's about."

Gordon gave Wade a long look. "You know, after reading all those files Rosenblatt had, about the Nazis here in Houston, I would have thought that would be bad. It is, but I have a thing now that I just can't put my finger on. Got a few minutes? I'd like to bend your ear, get your take on something."

"Sure," Wade said, "let's go back to my office. My real office."

He led the way to his inner office. On one wall stood three metal filing cabinets. On the opposite wall hung a calendar and a portrait of Franklin Roosevelt. The big wooden desk dominated the room. There were two chairs sitting opposite the desk. Wade plopped into one and motioned Gordon to take the other.

"You're a P.I.," Gordon said. "You got any liquid refreshment?"

"Gordie, not every real life P.I. stashes a bottle of hooch in his desk for late-night meetings. It's not like your stories."

"So that's a no?"

Wade stood. "Of course not. Whiskey or gin?"

"Whiskey would be great."

Wade prepared two glasses. Gordon downed his in one gulp.

"That bad, huh?" Wade poured more whiskey into Gordon's glass.

"Potentially."

"Lay it on me."

Gordon took a deep breath and started talking. He began with the assignment from Levitz, the secondary assignment to Bruno Clavell, and then his meeting with Victor's family. He made sure to mention that, with Victor gone, Naomi would have to do something about her mother.

"That got my ire up," Gordon said.

"And I know plenty well what happens when you get your ire up."

"Something had to make Victor believe he was seeing phantom automobiles," Gordon went on. That led him to Kermit Kernow, especially with the meds stolen. But that was a dead end. From there, he described how he began looking into Victor Tompkins's last days, including the meeting with Victor's employer, his excursion into Montgomery County, the run-in with the first car and the bullet hole in Victor's car.

"Look, Wade, folks just don't shoot at cars for no reason. Victor saw something out there and, well, there was that maroon car trying to run him down."

"You only assume it was running him down. Maybe that farmer didn't really see what he thought he saw."

"Sure, but then how does Victor start thinking there are spectral automobiles driving around town?"

"Beats me. The supernatural isn't in my jurisdiction."

Once Gordon got going, he forgot the whiskey. "I still think it has something to do with Kernow. What kind of medicine does a shrink give a man?"

"Haven't the foggiest."

Gordon bit his lip. "Be that as it may, we still have oddities. Peter Kingsbury is the driver who kills Victor by running him down. Kingsbury is an armored car driver who has the Amherst Bank on his route. His coworker said Kingsbury needed some extra cash. There were no skid marks on the pavements. That got me to thinking it might not have been an accident.

Wade leaned back. "What do the cops say about it?"

"Well, that's the thing. They don't say anything."

"Really? Who caught the Tompkins case?"

"Burt Wheeler."

Wade made a face that looked like he smelled something bad. "He's not the best. Even when I was a patrol cop, we all knew which detectives needed hand-holding. Wheeler was one."

"He dirty?"

"Not that I know of. More like clueless. Dense even. He's most likely to zero in on the quickest and easiest answer and, like a bulldog, latch on and never let go. Which means that if you have any hope of dislodging him to see things your way, you're gonna have to have a mountain of proof. Where you at with that?"

Gordon scratched the back of his neck and put on a sheepish grin. "Actually, as far as Wheeler's concerned, the case is closed."

"You're kidding, right?"

"Nope."

"Damn, Gordon, you don't make it easy, do you?"

"Guess not."

"What kind of proof do you have?"

Gordon eyed his glass. "None. I don't even know what to do next."

Wade slapped the desk. "The answer's simple: you need proof that something is going on."

"What's going on, then? What am I not seeing?"

"The connection. You need the one thing that ties it all together. I got a theory."

"Lay it on me."

Wade paused and swirled the whiskey in his glass. "Put another hat on for me. If this were one of those stories you write for those pulp magazines, how would you write it?"

Gordon shrugged. "Well, I tend to think big, like Doc Savage big. I thought this kind of thing was only fiction until I learned about the Nazis here in Houston. But small scale, I don't know. Maybe have Tompkins see something nefarious out in the woods, completely by accident, but that's enough to get him killed. The bad guys try to do it on the spot but fail. Then they follow Tompkins back to Houston and finish the job."

Wade nodded. "When you tell me all this stuff about Tompkins, there's one thing that gives me pause: you end up at that bank and Johnny Flynn is there also. And he's there because of his assigned story, the death of that artist. What's the common thread between the two?"

Gordon arched an eyebrow. "Kingsbury?"

"Say it with confidence, man. Kingsbury ran down your victim but he also has a connection, tenuous at best, with the dead artist. Now, what do you know about

Kingsbury?"

"Not a lot. One of his coworkers said he needed some extra cash." Gordon gaped at Wade. "Wait, are you thinking Kingsbury was hired to kill Tompkins and Silber?"

"That not what I'm saying. But I am saying it has a thread of a chance. Tompkins sees something out in the next county. A few days later, he ends up dead. He's killed by a car driven by Kingsbury. Someone also tried to kill him by car out in Montgomery County. Now, if you're writing this story, you have Kingsbury behind the wheel in both places. You, however, in the real world, can't say that. But there is something you can do."

"Find out more about Kingsbury." Gordon snapped his fingers. "But that still doesn't explain why Tompkins thought the cars were phantoms."

"Can't help you there. Maybe the answer lies with Kingsbury."

"Or Kernow. I still think he's involved."

"Maybe so. What do you know about the artist?"

Gordon spread his hands. "Nothing. Wasn't ever my story."

"And I bet Johnny won't let you in on it. By the way, what are you going to do if you find any evidence, go to your editor or the police?"

"Not sure if I'll even have a job tomorrow."

"That gonna stop you?"

"Not at all." Gordon stood. "Thanks, pal. You helped clear my mind. You on a case?"

Wade sighed and stood. "Actually, yes. Tail job. Gotta follow a cheating husband, snap some pictures, get them developed, and deliver the bill to the angry wife. What about you? Where you headed?"

"Back to the police station. I need to ask about Silber, get some details about his death. Maybe there's a connection. Then I'll look into Kingsbury."

Wade motioned to Gordon's glass still half-full with his second shot. "Gonna finish?"

Gordon grinned. "Nah. Don't need it now."

CHAPTER NINETEEN

The desk sergeant looked up, saw Gordon walking to his desk, and sighed. "Isn't three times a day a little excessive?"

Gordon spread his arms. "Mike, c'mon, don't you enjoy the press?"

"No. What do you want?"

Gordon sauntered up to the counter and leaned an elbow on it. "A little nugget of knowledge, if you don't mind." He glanced at his watch. "I know it's after five, but do you know which detective caught the William Silber murder case and, if so, is he here?"

Mike tapped his pencil on the desk. "Don't know and don't know."

"Mikey, this is me we're talking about."

"I know. You're the guy who leaves Myrna Loy alone on the dance floor, and that's the least of your problems this week."

"I'm working on something big."

"You're always working on something big."

"What'll it take for you to slide me that information?"

Mike thought a moment. "How about the name of that photographer lady you were with earlier today? She's a real beauty."

Gordon thought a moment. "Sure. You dish then I'll

dish."

Keeping his eye on Gordon, Mike picked up the phone and talked with someone on the other end. He tapped his pencil. "Thank you." He hung up. "I got the name."

"Dish."

"Burt Wheeler."

Gordon's flashy grin faded a bit. "Are you serious?"

Mike's grin got a lot bigger. "Sure am. And the lady?"

"Lucy Barnes." Gordon slipped his elbow off the desk.

The door to the inner office banged open. Burt Wheeler stood in its frame, a cigarette dangling from his lips. "Gardner, what the hell are you doing? Digging your grave deeper?"

"Detective Wheeler," Gordon said, "so good to see you again. And before you ask, this isn't about the other thing. It's about the artist, Silber."

"What about him? I already talked with Johnny. Why the hell you asking about him?" He came to stand at the desk sergeant's desk.

"Background."

"On what?"

"My piece on Bruno Clavell."

Wheeler narrowed his eyes. "How's that work?"

"I've been assigned a story to cover Clavell's new nightclub. It's a puff piece on Clavell. Silber plays a role."

"How?"

How indeed. Gordon put his pulp fiction mind to work. "Silber was commissioned by Clavell to do some interior artwork for the nightclub. Turns out Clavell likes to decorate his nightclubs with some local flavor and hires artists from the area to do the work."

"And your point is?"

"Mr. Clavell, in my interview with him today, was asking about Silber's death. You know, the circumstances and such. I'll be seeing him again tonight. Thought I'd swing by here and get some details."

Wheeler loosened his already loose tie. "He can read about it in the paper tomorrow."

Gordon held up his index finger. "Sure thing, but what's the gist? So I can tell Clavell tonight when I see him. He likes to know things ahead of the average joe."

Wheeler sighed. "It's a pretty open-and-shut case." He fished out a crumpled pack of cigarettes and lit one using his lighter. "If I tell you, will you just go away?"

Gordon crossed his heart. "I promise."

Wheeler squinted. "Ain't much to it. According to his wife, the bank was his last big project. He had a couple other commissions he was getting to. He got a call from a potential client to paint the ship channel for some place or other. Not sure about that. That's why he was down in that part of town where he was mugged. No one saw anything, but his pockets were all cleaned out. No one even heard the gunshots that killed him. Must've used a silencer."

Gordon frowned. "What kind of mugger uses a silencer?"

"One that doesn't want to be found."

"Any leads?"

"None."

Gordon looked skeptical. "Nothing?"

Wheeler ran his fingers through his hair. The Brylcreem was already worn off by the day's work. "Not really."

"Wait a moment. 'Not really' means you have something but don't know where it fits. Whatcha got?"

Wheeler looked annoyed. He stabbed out his cigarette in the ashtray on the desk. Mike didn't even hide the fact he was listening in. A few patrol cops wandered in and out of the station.

Gordon took a step closer. "What is it?" he whispered.

Wheeler almost didn't speak. "The client. The one who asked Silber to paint a picture of the ship channel. We talked with him in his house. He felt really bad about Silber's death, you know. Like it was his fault or something. It wasn't, but he thought that anyway. He kept going on and on about the bad timing and such."

Gordon could tell Wheeler was sticking on a fact. Perhaps the big lug had the makings of a decent detective after all. "What's got you pausing, Burt?"

Wheeler shook it off. "Doesn't matter. It's got no bearing on the case. The fact of the matter is that Silber was mugged and killed for whatever goddamn money that was in his wallet. And we ain't no closer to finding the guys who did than we were last week."

Gordon waited a few beats to let Wheeler's temper subside. "Burt, something's got under your skin. What is it?"

"Yeah, Burt," Mike said, "spill."

Wheeler eyed Mike and then Gordon, squinting at both men. "I don't know. It's gonna sound funny. Promise me y'all won't laugh?"

Both men nodded.

"It's just that the paintings on this guy's walls in his house. They were all of country scenes and stuff. None of the paintings were cities or modern things and all."

Gordon waited for more but nothing came.

Wheeler slammed his open palm on the desk. Mike jumped. So did Gordon. "Dammit, that's why I never wanted to say anything."

"What?" Gordon asked. "What are you thinking?"

"Why would a guy commission Silber to paint the ship channel when every other painting in his house is country, woody stuff?"

Gordon didn't see the connection. "I'm not sure. Out of curiosity, what was the guy's name?"

"Joseph Dickson. Know him?"

"Nope. You?"

"Nah."

"What's he do?"

"Operates an armored car company."

Gordon frowned. "Armored car company. That's interesting."

"What?"

"Not sure. Might just be a coincidence. Then again maybe not. It just seems funny that in all of my investigation on the Tompkins story, I've now got two instances of armored car companies. And you know what goes with armored cars?"

"Money," both policemen said almost in unison.

"Absolutely. Now we're getting somewhere."

Wheeler shook his head.

Gordon could tell thoughts were racing around behind the thick forehead.

"Probably just a coincidence. We got no leads for Silber's murder and the Tompkins case is saucer and blown. Without evidence, we've got nothing."

Gordon put on his hat.

"Where you going?" Wheeler said.

"To find some evidence. Wanna come with me?"

Wheeler glanced at Mike, then at Gordon. He hesitated an instant. "Nah, I'm going home. My day's done."

"Suit yourself," Gordon said. "Mine's just getting started."

CHAPTER TWENTY

Gordon Gardner parked his car in front of Peter Kingsbury's house and paused. In the past half-hour, he had called in a favor and got the name and address of Gonzales Securities, the company Joseph Dickson owned. No connection jumped out at him, so he resolved himself to grilling Kingsbury with as many questions as it took to find answers. Gordon had an internal debate whether to just come out and accuse Kingsbury of killing Tompkins or go about it diplomatically. He opened the car door and decided to let Kingsbury have some rope and see if he'd hang himself.

Walking up the sidewalk, Gordon wished Wade were with him or even Lucy. Not that she could do much but, if Kingsbury was a killer, what would stop him from taking out Gordon and then her?

Nothing. Absolutely nothing. Gordon swallowed, his throat suddenly dry. But what alternative did he have? Without evidence, Wheeler would do nothing. Without evidence or a connection, Levitz would do nothing. Hell, Gordon was probably out of a job tomorrow any way. Might as well go out in a blaze of glory.

Kingsbury's neighborhood was nice and quaint, with nice houses and nice front yards all mowed and edged to perfection. Norman Rockwell wasn't this perfect. At early evening, just after dusk, a few folks were out walking. A young couple strolled hand in hand. An image flashed through Gordon's head of him and Lucy doing the same thing. He shook his head and refocused.

Several cars were parked along the streets, others were in driveways. The sky was a dark blue as twilight turned to night. Lights along most houses had already turned on for the night. It was pretty much the same as Gordon's own neighborhood.

Gordon made a fist and knocked on the front door. It eased open a crack, hinges creaking.

The first thing that shot into Gordon's mind was to turn around and call Wheeler. Or Wade. Suspicious men didn't leave their doors unlocked. But what if it was nothing? What if all his ideas about Kingsbury and his involvement in whatever was going on amounted to nothing? If Gordon was going to convince anyone there was a story here, he needed the story first.

Careful not to leave fingerprints, Gordon used his shoe to open the door farther. "Mr. Kingsbury?" he called out into the house. No answer. He stepped inside.

The living room was spare, most likely indicating Kingsbury lived alone. The den, however, was a mess. Sofa cushions were overturned and ripped open. A lamp, still illuminated, lay on the floor, and the drawers of a desk were pulled out and the contents tossed onto the floor. In the air, there was an odor of a recent fire and Gordon noticed smoldering ashes in the fireplace. *Who would use the fireplace in the spring?*

"Mr. Kingsbury, are you here? It's Gordon Gardner, the reporter."

"Then you're gonna write your own obituary." The man's voice was Kingsbury's.

Reflexively, Gordon paused and spread out his arms.

He turned around and saw Kingsbury standing in a corner. In his hand, he held a revolver.

"What happened here?" Gordon said.

Kingsbury sniffed. "They came looking for it." A little grin etched itself across his mouth. "They didn't find it."

Gordon looked down and saw a suitcase. "What didn't they find?"

"Why are you here?"

"To get the whole story."

"What story do you think you have?"

Gordon was very aware of the gun still pointed at him. "Can you point that away?"

Kingsbury relaxed and lowered the gun. "Sure. You ain't them."

"Who are you talking about?"

"You can't print anything about this in the paper, you know. It's too big."

Gordon was getting frustrated with all the questions and no answers. "Look, Mr. Kingsbury, I only have pieces. I don't have anything that ties things together. The only common piece is you. That's why I'm here."

The hand holding the gun rose again. It aimed at Gordon's stomach. "That's what I was afraid of. You know too much."

"I don't know anything," Gordon snapped, "but I'm beginning to find out. Let me tell you what I think."

"Surprise me."

"I think you killed Victor Tompkins because of what he saw out in Montgomery County. Now, whether you were put up to it, I don't know, but the physical evidence at the scene of the crime indicated you didn't try to swerve or stop. Thus, you ran him down. That's murder. But I don't know why."

"And you ain't ever gonna." Kingsbury raised the gun higher to fire.

From the rear of the house, a door was kicked in. The momentary distraction was enough for Gordon to dive to the floor. He could hold his own in a fistfight for a while but he couldn't fight an armed man. Besides, good guys never kicked down doors.

He landed on the wooden floor near the overturned lamp.

Kingsbury immediately forgot Gordon. He muttered, "Aw, hell," and moved to the next room. From other parts of the house, heavy footsteps pounded on the floor.

Gordon spied the open front door and got his feet under him for the sprint. A slip of paper just under the couch caught his eye. It had a distinctive shape, one he easily recognized. He grabbed it and put it in his jacket pocket.

Two shots were fired.

A man grunted.

A body thunked to the floor.

The footsteps continued to move forward.

Gordon Gardner broke into a dead run. He cleared the front doorway, never looking back. He plunged his hand into his pocket while running and came up with his keys. He threw open the door and roared his car to life. Ignoring anything in the rearview mirrors, he put the car into gear and peeled out, leaving rubber on the road. He missed the few cars parked along the street and turned as soon as he could. He wanted to put as much distance as possible between him and the shooting.

He drove wildly, nearly out of control until he left the neighborhood. Police would be coming soon. When they figured out who the likely dead man was, they'd come looking for him.

"How the hell you going to explain that, Mister Ace Reporter?" Gordon muttered to himself.

Then he had his answer, the only answer that mattered. "With the whole story."

He reached into his jacket pocket and pulled out the slip of paper. It was a small band banks used to wrap stacks of money. On one side of the strip was the amount: $1,000.

Gordon turned it over.

"Gonzales Securities."

CHAPTER TWENTY-ONE

Lucy Barnes put her key in the door of her apartment. She was nearly inside when Gordon Gardner stepped from behind a planter. She screamed and nearly dropped the flat satchel she carried. "Good Lord, Ace, you scared the dickens out of me."

No one was in the open walkway at five minutes to midnight. "Come on, let's get inside."

Gordon followed her. In the moments before she turned on the lights, they were in near total darkness. He smelled the odor of the developing chemicals on her clothes mixed with her perfume.

She switched on a lamp. Warm light oozed into the room. It was tastefully furnished with a couch, coffee table, chair and end table. A kitchen table and chair sat next to the wall. The kitchenette was small. One door led to her bedroom, the other indicated the bathroom.

Lucy read his thoughts. "It came fully furnished." She put her bag down on the coffee table and stared at Gordon. "Where've you been, Ace? You don't look so good."

Gordon straightened his already straight tie. "Hiding. Running. Trying to figure out what to do next." He plopped down into the chair. "Lucy, I heard a man get shot tonight."

"I know. I heard."

Gordon looked up at her sharply. "How?"

She eased down onto the couch and slipped off her shoes. "Word filtered down to the darkroom when I was developing those pictures. It was Kingsbury, right?"

"Yeah," he said. "I didn't do it. You gotta believe me."

"I do. What happened?"

"I was talking with him and he was about to tell me more of the story when some toughs broke in the back door. Kingsbury went to confront them and got himself shot. I'm guessing he didn't make it."

She shook her head. "The police came around the newsroom looking for you. They called you a person of interest but I'm guessing they were going to haul you in."

"That's why I've kept away from the newsroom and my house. I figured they're both being watched. I've been here for two hours, in case someone was following you."

She arched an eyebrow. "So you led them here?" A mischievous grin etched her mouth.

"Don't think so. I stashed my car over at Grand Central. I caught a cab, then two more. I had no way to contact my friend, the private eye, so I thought the next best place was to come here."

"To a single lady's apartment. What will the neighbors think?"

"You know your neighbors?"

"Nope."

"Then you don't care."

"Pretty much." She leaned over and grabbed the bag. "But I've got something you need to see." She patted the spot on the couch next to her. "C'mon, let me show you."

He slipped next to her. His nose picked up a stronger sense of her, primarily her perfume. For a moment, his head swam. Gordon had the presence of mind to acknowledge how good she still looked at midnight. He refocused as she opened the bag.

Lucy pulled out a sheaf of file folders. She placed them on the coffee table and opened one. Inside were black-and-white photographs.

He picked one up. "Is this Montgomery County? Can't believe that was earlier today. Seems like last week."

"Long days can do that to you." She started flipping through them until she found the one she wanted. "Look at this one."

Gordon held the photograph in his hands. It showed the road heading up over the rise, the dense woods on both sides, and their shadows on the ground. "Okay, I'm looking. What am I supposed to be seeing?"

She leaned in, pointing at something on the right of the photograph. "That. What does that look like to you?"

He narrowed his eyes, peering closer. What she indicated looked regular and orderly. "It looks like some sort of shadow or branch roughly in the shape of a triangle."

Riffling through her other photographs, she produced another and handed it to him. "I thought so, too, so I enlarged it. Here. Now tell me what you see."

In the second image, the triangle filled the page. With the higher resolution, the triangle took on a more obvious look. It appeared less natural and more man-made, especially with all the environment surrounding it.

"I'm seeing what appears to be not a branch or a shadow but a what?" He held both the enlarged photo and the original in front of him, comparing them both. Once he saw the dark triangle, he couldn't miss it. "Wait a minute," he muttered, looking at the original. "What's this?" He ran his finger in a half-circle over part of the picture above the shadowy triangle.

"C'mon, Ace, do I have to do your work for you?" Lucy kidded. "Forget what you're seeing and just tell me what you think it looks like."

He frowned, the words not exactly coming easily. "I'm seeing an arch, an arch in the woods. But we didn't see it when we were there."

"Because we weren't supposed to see it. No one was ever supposed to see it. Don't you get it? It's camouflaged."

"What's camouflaged?"

"I did some measurements of this original to try to get a sense of the size of this arch. Based on my calculations, it's about eight feet tall and about six feet wide."

"Holy cow, that's huge. Why that's big enough to…" He paused, mouth opening wide, looking at her.

Almost in unison, they said, "To drive a car through."

Gordon put both pictures down, side by side, on the table. His mind raced with the possibilities. He stood and started pacing. Every now and then he glanced back at the picture.

"It's like those kinds of optical illusions that you can't see until someone shows you what to look at and then you can't not see it. No wonder Tompkins thought he saw a car disappear. To his mind, he really did."

Lucy stood. "But that's silly. If I see a car disappear into the woods, I'm going to investigate."

"I know, and that's probably what Victor did. But someone tried to scare him away by shooting at his car. They missed and actually ended up messing up his car."

"And then they tried to run him down."

"They almost got him, but Bob Hastings came along the road and stopped it."

Lucy started pacing as well. "But it doesn't explain why he thought other cars were phantoms?"

Gordon bit his lip. "Yeah, I know." He sifted through everything he had learned in the past two days. When he was on a story, he would make a point to stop and replay the sequence of events in order. That was how he happened upon...

"The medicine." He whirled and faced Lucy. "It's the only explanation. Whatever medicine he was taking for whatever ailed him had to be the reason he kept thinking cars were phantoms."

"What kind of medicine makes that happen?"

"Not sure." Gordon pulled out his notebook and flipped through the pages. "We'll have to ask Kernow again. Or the doctor up in Montgomery. What was his name?" He stopped flipping and started reading his notes, running his finger across the pages. "Oh my."

"What?"

"The doctor up in Montgomery County? His name is Stephen Dickson."

"Yeah, so?"

Gordon plunged his hand into his pocket and pulled out the money wrapper. He handed it to her. "I found that at Kingsbury's house."

She turned it over in her hands. "I'm not seeing the connection."

"Gonzales Securities is owned and operated by Joseph Dickson."

Lucy cocked her head. "You don't think they're related?"

Slowly, Gordon nodded his head. "Can't say for sure but it's too much of a coincidence." Something clicked in his mind and a whole world of realization flooded in on him. "No way," he muttered to himself. "It can't be."

"What?" Lucy stepped closer to him. "Tell me."

"We've been forgetting to ask another question. Who made the camouflage?"

"It's good work," she said. "Very realistic."

"Exactly. The kind of work made by an excellent artist. An artist commissioned to paint some sort of camouflage that is so big you can drive a car through. An artist who was commissioned by one Joseph Dickson to paint the ship channel but was mugged and killed instead. An artist named…"

"William Silber," Lucy said. "The one who painted the mural in the bank."

"The bank where Peter Kingsbury was an armored car driver," Gordon said.

"My gosh, Ace, what have we stumbled on?"

Gordon Gardner got a million-dollar grin on his face. "Another front-page story."

CHAPTER TWENTY-TWO

Gordon Gardner knocked on the front door of another normal house in a normal neighborhood. It was nearly one in the morning and he furtively looked up and down the street. He and Lucy were the only people moving. The glow of the street lamps could be seen over the roofs of the houses on this little stretch of street.

"Now who is this again?" Lucy asked.

"Colby Burke," Gordon said. "He's a veteran of the Great War. Grew up out in San Marcos, near Austin. His dad was a mechanic for the railroads and passed along the love of engines to Colby. Now, when you see him, you'll notice one of the two reasons we're here."

Footsteps shuffled behind the door. A light came on. A key entered the lock. The door opened and Colby Burke's enormous bulk filled the door frame.

"Hi, Colby."

"Gordon? What the hell are you doing here? Do you know what time it is?"

"It's one."

Colby looked at Lucy. She had changed into khakis, a denim shirt, and hiking boots. "And who is this?"

"Lucy Barnes, meet Colby Burke. You think we could come in? I've got something to lay on you and I'd like your help."

Burke opened the door for them to enter. Lucy gasped

in astonishment at the mounted and stuffed animals on the walls.

"Oh, I forgot to mention," Gordon said, "Colby's a big game hunter. He's handy with a rifle. That's the other reason we're here."

Burke stood in the entryway and looked down on Gordon. Six-feet-four, Colby wore striped pajamas and house shoes. He ran his fingers through his brown hair, making most of it lie down correctly. "You know I was sleeping, right?"

"Yeah, but you'll love this one. I've got a story that I need an ending to, but to get there, I'm gonna need some help."

"What kind of help?" Burke shuffled across the room and turned on an overhead light.

Lucy stared in wonderment. Nearly every square foot of wall space featured some sort of animal, from fish to birds to bears and everything in between.

"Did you kill all of them?"

Burke beamed with pride. "Yes, ma'am. I've hunted on six continents in over four dozen countries. If it's huntable, I want to hunt it."

"How about bank robbers and murderers?" Gordon asked. "You ever hunted them?"

Burke slowly turned his head. "What have you gotten yourself into?"

"A lot. But I can get out with your help. Only thing is, um, you can't mount their heads on your wall."

"Why not? If they're murderers, don't they deserve that?"

"Possibly, but the police and the courts might not think so. C'mon, let me tell you a story."

A half-hour later, as they sat around the kitchen table drinking coffee, Gordon finished his tale. Lucy had chimed in at certain points and showed her photographs.

"I've been in deer blinds that don't look that good. You say an artist painted that?"

"That's our suspicion."

"And where's your proof?"

Gordon looked at Lucy. "Well, that's our sticking point. With Kingsbury murdered and me most likely out of a job tomorrow, the only thing to do is to find the evidence and then present it in one fell swoop. That way, we can save my job, get Lucy a page-one photo, and you can have another war story for your collection."

"You intrigue me, Gordon, I'll give you that. So what's your plan?"

Gordon told him. The more Gordon talked, the wider Burke's smile became. "I'm in. Let me get dressed." He rose and went into his bedroom.

"Do you really think it'll work?" Lucy asked.

Gordon shrugged. "It's the best option of few good ones."

"And you don't think we should go to the police with this?"

"And tell them what? That we think we know who killed Tompkins and Silber because of a camouflaged driveway out in Montgomery County? They wouldn't give us the time of day. No, the only way someone like

Detective Wheeler is going to believe us is if we serve it to him on a silver tray." He downed the last of his coffee. "Listen, if you're worried about any of this, Colby and I can go. You can stay here."

"And miss all the fun?" She arched her eyebrow. "I haven't enjoyed myself this much in a long, long time. I was just making sure going it alone is the best course of action."

Burke came back into the kitchen. He wore heavy khaki pants and shirt, a hunting vest, and a fedora. Over his shoulder was slung a rifle. "The cops can be hampered by law. We're not. I'm ready. We'll take my truck since I can drive on dirt." He pointed at Gordon. "You want a weapon?"

Gordon thought a moment then shook his head. "I'm still press. So is she. That's why we have you."

"Fine. Let's go."

CHAPTER TWENTY-THREE

"This is just like the time I hunted alligator down in Florida," Colby Burke said.

"Except this time," Gordon said, "the prey might shoot back."

Burke shrugged. "I'll just have to duck."

The trio traipsed along the country road on foot, nearing the spot where Victor Tompkins had nearly been run down by a maroon car. The first pink light of dawn filtered through the tall pine trees and dense underbrush. Their footwear quickly became damp with the morning dew.

Burke had done a drive-by without headlights while Lucy pinpointed the general area. She couldn't be sure in the dark, but used the last known country house up the road as a marker. Once Burke was satisfied with the area, he parked his pickup over the rise along the side of the road.

"This has a real George Washington-crossing-the-Delaware feel to it." Gordon brought up the rear.

Lucy, with her camera satchel over her shoulder, marched between the two men. "Except we're not in a boat."

"Or with an army," Burke said.

"That's not what I meant," Gordon said. "I mean the idea that if the bank robbers are there, they'll likely be asleep."

"How do you figure that?" Burke asked.

"With this camouflaged entrance, no one can see what's going on in the road. Without the fear of being caught, I bet those bank robbers sleep real easy."

"If I was sitting on a bunch of moolah with a hiding place as good as this," Burke said, "so would I." He motioned them closer to the tree line, then made a hand gesture for them to crouch. "If what Miss Barnes's picture shows, we're close. I want to make sure there isn't a sentry on guard. Then I'll…"

From over the rise came the shine of headlights. They came from the opposite direction from where Burke had parked his truck.

"Quick," said the big man, "into the trees."

Almost as one, the three of them scurried into the trees and underbrush. Limbs cracked and leaves rustled as their footfalls tramped the ground.

The car topped the rise and crested it. The twin headlights pierced the darkness. The tires burred over the country lane's asphalt.

The car slowed; the three of them crouched lower. The bulk of the car came into view. The ambient glow of dawn combined with the headlights allowed Gordon to make out the shape of the vehicle. "A '38 Oldsmobile," he whispered to Lucy.

She nodded.

The Olds slowed further and turned to what appeared to be solid dense forest. With some slight maneuvering, the driver eased the car forward. Now that they knew what to look for, the trio saw the automobile part what appeared to be a large canvas tarp, very much like a circus tent. The headlights illuminated the painted surface but there were also real branches and leaves affixed to the tarp as well. The optical illusion was remarkable. The Olds, for all intents and purposes, simply vanished from the road.

"Well, I'll be damned," Burke murmured. "I have to admit I only half believed you, Gordon."

"What? Then why did you come?"

"For the fun."

With the area mostly dark, the headlights illuminated the structure from the inside, making it glow. It appeared to be a short, covered bridge, about thirty feet long. Within moments, the headlights showed the open back of the structure, then the vehicle emerged out the other side, driving slowly along the hidden driveway, tires crunching gravel.

"Let's go," Gordon said. "Get your camera ready, Lucy. No flash."

"Naturally, Ace," Lucy said. She unbuckled her satchel and took out her camera. "Ready."

They crept along just inside the tree line for the remaining few feet until they arrived at the camouflaged opening. Seeing it up close, even in the growing light of dawn, impressed Gordon. "Look how Silber painted it to appear real even up this close. The man was a genius."

"Wonder why he did it?" Lucy mused.

"Y'all can admire the art later," Burke whispered.

"Now, let's just get ourselves in position." He unslung his rifle and used the barrel to move one of the camouflaged flaps. Satisfied no danger lurked, he ducked in. Gordon and Lucy followed.

Car exhaust, animal droppings, and a damp wooden smell hit their noses. "Guess they didn't need smell camouflage," Lucy said. "It reeks like a bunch of animals used this as their outhouse."

"It's a nice, safe environment for them," Burke said.

They crept slowly up the winding road. To mask it from being seen, the ground was coated with dry pine needles. The trio hugged the edge of the road, stooping and crouching inch-by-inch until Burke, with a hand gesture, motioned them down on their haunches. They leaned in as he whispered. "House and barn up ahead. Two cars, one delivery truck. Armored. That fit with your theory?"

Gordon shrugged. "Mostly. Maybe they switch out the trucks when they rob the banks. Lucy, get a shot."

Nodding, Lucy stood and framed the scene. Her finger pushed the button and the camera clicked. The sound was like a twig snapping. She quickly lowered herself to the ground. "I forgot how loud the clicks are."

"No bother." Burke never took his gaze off the house. "No one heard."

"Wrong, buster," a man's voice said behind them. "Someone did hear." The sound of a rifle jacking a round in place jolted the sudden silence. "Don't move. I've got you covered. You, with the rifle, drop it."

Burke opened his mitts and his rifle fell to the ground.

He put his hands over his head. Gordon and Lucy did likewise.

"Now, let's go see the boss."

CHAPTER TWENTY-FOUR

Hands up, Gordon, Lucy, and Burke trudged in front of the rifleman who had picked up Burke's rifle and slung it over his shoulder. Lucy's camera bag swung at her waist. They approached an old house and barn. No other person could be seen, but there was a faint humming sound coming from inside the barn. The tall pine trees and dense foliage killed all sight lines. If Gordon hadn't already known the direction of the road, he could have easily gotten lost.

"Didn't see that coming, did you?" Burke muttered to Gordon.

"No, but it makes sense. Tompkins's car was shot at. My guess is it was our friend back there, standing guard. Didn't think the lookout spot would have been on top of that contraption."

"Shut up." The rifleman guided them around the house to the area between the rear of the house and the barn. "Okay, stop right there."

They stopped.

A moment later, a man dressed in overalls and boots exited the house. He stopped in his tracks. "What the hell is this, Meyer?"

"Found 'em snooping at the front door. They was taking pictures. Better get Mr. Dickson."

The other man in overalls nodded and walked into the barn. He returned with two more men. One was dressed similarly to him; the other was decked out in a brown suit and tie. His hat was cantered at a rakish angle.

The suited man approached the trio. "Well, well, well, what do we have here?" He peered up at Burke, let his eyes rove invitingly over Lucy then fixed on Gordon. The man put a finger to his lips and thought a moment. "You look familiar."

"So do you," Gordon said. "Family resemblance being what it is, I'm guessing you're Joseph Dickson. I believe your brother, Stephen, works at the hospital up here in this county. We talked with him yesterday."

Dickson snapped his fingers. "Right. You're that reporter who landed in the *Tribune* yesterday. Gardner, right?"

Despite his situation, Gordon liked being recognized. He bowed with his head as if he were an actor taking a curtain call. "Gordon Gardner, *Houston Post-Dispatch*."

"I've read your stuff. You're good. Too bad you won't get a chance to write this one."

Gordon chuckled. "Actually, you're wrong. I've already written it. Back in Houston."

Dickson smiled. "Unlikely. Why would y'all be sneaking around up here if you knew everything?"

"Evidence. We know what's going on and we know y'all've killed at least two people to keep the secret."

The smile faded from Dickson's face. "Then you know we won't have a qualm about killing three more." Something in his cheek twitched. "Out of curiosity, what do you think we're doing?"

Gordon shifted his feet. "Can we put our hands down?"

Dickson gave an indifferent shrug.

Gordon inhaled deeply to clear away his fear. "You're Joseph Dickson, owner of Gonzales Securities. You transport cash and other valuables to and from banks. Naturally, you have business rivals including Lone Star Armored Truck Service. Wanting to get an edge, you would naturally want to infiltrate your rivals, peel off one of them, and start to undermine those other companies from within. Victor Tompkins happened to see something he wasn't supposed to—the driving of your cars through that camouflaged entrance. You had to make sure he didn't talk.

"I'm guessing your brother's in on it, too. He's likely the one who gave Tompkins some sort of drug that made him not believe his own eyes. Made him a victim of suggestion. Made him think he was crazy. Then, of course, you killed off your killer, Kingsbury, so he wouldn't talk either. How I'm doing so far?"

Dickson shook his head. "How do you make a living as a reporter? You're only half right. But, it doesn't matter any way. You won't live to correct your errors."

"Errors?" Gordon said. "I found one of the money wrappers in Kingsbury's house. It was from your firm. What the hell errors did I make?"

Dickson nodded to the barn. "It's in there. You're tenacious, I'll give you that. Might as well let you know where you were wrong before I shoot you and your friends in the head."

Gordon gulped. Some of his bravado evaporated. He suddenly wished he had asked Wade to come along. The private eye carried a collapsible baton for use in close combat. Gordon, being a press member, carried nothing of the kind.

He eyed Burke. The big man's expression was unreadable.

With Meyer still training his rifle on their backs, Gordon, Lucy, and Burke followed Dickson into the barn. Immediately Gordon and Lucy looked at each other; they knew the odor. It wasn't hay or feed or anything related to a barn. It was mechanical and something else.

"Ink?" they asked in unison.

"Yes, Mr. Gardner, ink."

"What are you doing, making a newspaper?"

"Not a newspaper." Dickson moved out of the way to let Gordon see.

Three tables were centered in the room. On each table, small presses were running, creating the sound Gordon had heard from outside. The pieces of paper coming off the presses were instantly recognizable.

"Counterfeit," Gordon breathed. The last piece of the puzzle chinked into place. "Of course! That's why the banks never reported anything missing. For all they knew, nothing was missing." He turned to Dickson. "That means the money Kingsbury had in his house wasn't sourdough. He was escaping with real money."

"My money," Dickson growled. "He was stealing my money."

"That must mean you have at least one employee for every armored car firm here in town on your payroll. Or blackmail."

"Blackmail's cheaper." Some of Dickson's more pleasant demeanor was returning. "Take them out back and finish them. If he knows about us, that means he's been talking. Time to pack up and move."

Meyer marched the three of them back outside and around behind the barn. There was a pile of chopped wood along the rear wall. A small trail led down a ditch.

"Down there," Meyer said.

To his two companions, Gordon said, "Sorry I dragged y'all into this."

"Don't be," Burke said. "It was still fun."

"Yeah, Ace." Lucy's voice quavered a bit. "Thanks for showing a girl the time of her life."

"Stop yer yammering and git down there," Meyer said.

Gordon paused, looked at Burke, then Lucy. He opened his mouth to say something.

Meyer raised his rifle to shoot.

From the front of the barn, they heard Dickson shout a warning. All four of them came up short. A second cry punctuated the first. That was all Gordon and Burke needed.

Gordon pushed Lucy, throwing her to the ground.

Burke dropped to his haunches and swung his leg behind him. His booted foot connected with Meyer's shin. The gunman grunted in surprise and pain. He brought the rifle to bear on Burke, ready to fire point blank into the big man. Gordon, however, doing his best impression of a linebacker, plowed into Meyer.

The rifle cracked. Burke grunted.

Gordon found himself on top of the rifleman. In a flash, the thug backhanded Gordon across the mouth.

Stunned with the sharp pain, Gordon offered little resistance as Meyer scrambled to extricate himself. He pushed Gordon toward the barn, landing him hard on the wood pile.

Getting his feet under him, Meyer lashed out with a vicious kick directly into Burke's injured shoulder. The hunter let out another yelp of pain and grasped his shoulder with his free hand.

Meyer spent a second locating the rifle. He found it in Lucy's hands. She had gotten back up on her knees and grabbed it. She was turning it around to fire at Meyer when he reached out and took the butt in a beefy mitt. He yanked it and the weapon slipped from Lucy's hands. With practiced ease, he put the weapon into position.

Gordon recovered faster than he ever had in any previous fight. He shook his head to clear the cobwebs and took stock of the situation in a flash. Burke was down; Lucy had the rifle aimed at her middle. That only left him.

Clutching one of the pieces of wood from the pile, Gordon swung for the fences like Babe Ruth. He connected wood with Meyer's head. A sickening thunk brought the gunman down in a heap.

Gordon breathed heavily. His shirt was untucked and his suit coat ripped at the seam. "You okay?" he asked Lucy.

She nodded. Her hands shook.

"Colby?" Gordon asked peering down at his friend.

Burke eased up to a sitting position. "I'll live. Flesh wound. Hurts like the devil, though."

Lucy had the wherewithal to open her camera bag. She took out her camera and attached the flash, then inspected the device to verify it was still working properly. Doing something repetitive and productive leeched the fear out of her.

She held out her hand to Gordon. He took it and helped her to her feet. "C'mon, Ace, let's go get the rest of the story."

CHAPTER TWENTY-FIVE

Gordon and Lucy peered around the barn. What they saw they never expected to see.

Police lights snaked through the forest and foliage. Officers in both HPD and Montgomery County sheriff's uniforms moved around, securing both the house and the barn. The counterfeiters, who as recently as ten minutes ago had controlled everything, now stood in a group, hands above their heads. Some officers trained guns on them while others patted them down.

"That's a front-page shot." Lucy stepped out from behind the barn and snapped a photo.

Gordon, his hands bracketing an imaginary headline, said, "Cops Capture Counterfeiters by Gordon Gardner and Lucy Barnes."

She winked at Gordon. "Glad to get the byline with you, Ace."

One of the sheriff's deputies noticed the pair and turned his gun to them. "Freeze!"

Heads turned to see them.

"They're with me." Detective Burt Wheeler trundled from the pack of felons and officers. "You look terrible, Gardner."

"Burt!" Gordon rushed over and clasped hands with the detective. "Wait, what's going on here? How'd you get out here?"

Wheeler gave the reporter a playful, pitying look. "Gordon, I'm a detective. I followed you."

Gordon frowned. "From where?"

"From Lucy's place. I took a guess as to where you might go. Called up the paper and got her address. I guessed right. I sat on her street for hours. You took your damn sweet time getting there, too. Then you were in there for a while." He grinned conspiratorially. "What'd y'all do in there?"

"Nothing," Gordon said.

"We talked," Lucy said at the same time.

The two of them chuckled.

The detective eyed the pair. "Whatever. I followed you to that other guy's house. By the way, where is he?"

"Here," Burke said. He walked up to the group, bloody hand trying to staunch the flow from his wound. "Got a medic?"

"We'll call one," said a deputy.

Gordon said. "Oh there's another counterfeiter back there, too. Not sure how bad off he is."

"Pretty bad," Burke said. "Thanks, Gordo. I owe you one."

The two men shook hands.

Gordon eyed Wheeler. "I thought you didn't believe me."

"No, I told you we didn't have any leads. I had only heard about your style. I never got to see it up close. You were very passionate, bull-dogged, even. It got me to thinking." Burt tapped his forehead. "I can think, you know?"

"Never doubted it."

"Sure. I got to thinking about the case and what you said about coincidences. And I thought some more about Joseph Dickson and his commissioning that painting and Silber getting himself killed. Then I did something I'll swear I never did if my captain asks."

"What?"

"Used my imagination. I just asked myself what if you were right? What if Tompkins's death was a murder? That meant Kingsbury was the killer. I still didn't see it. Then this call comes in that there's been a shooting at Kingsbury's house. He's dead and multiple reports indicate two cars left the scene in a hurry. Being assigned to the Silber case and having heard what you said, I looked around Kingsbury's house. You wanna know what I found?"

Gordon pulled the money wrapper from his pocket. "More of these?"

Burt took the wrapper. "Yeah, actually. They were half-burned in his fireplace."

Gordon snapped his fingers. "Right. I smelled that."

"So that was you who drove away from the scene of a murder?" Wheeler's voice contained no humor.

"Um, yeah." Gordon sheepishly scratched the back of his neck. "I didn't want to get blamed."

Wheeler furtively looked around and lowered his voice. "Good call. But that's what got me thinking some more. I kinda figured it was you and wanted to get the straight talk from you, out in the wild and not in the police station. I went by your house but you never showed. That's when I got the idea you might be headed over to her place."

Both men glanced at Lucy. She was moving in and around all the activity, busily snapping pictures and framing the story. She noticed them looking at her and waved.

They waved back. "She's a real looker," Burt said.

"That she is. I might need to treat her to a proper date since our first one ended so unexpectedly."

"Try to stay out of the papers this time."

"Say," Gordon said, "did you happen to call my paper with any of this?"

Burt playfully slapped Gordon's shoulder. "Are you kidding? I barely had time to make the calls I made and sweet-talk my captain into this raid. Do you know how hard it is to do anything on a car radio while on a stakeout? But I think I've earned some points with him. Maybe I'll get a promotion."

"After being mentioned prominently in my story, most certainly. You're the one who solved these cases."

"Actually, it was you."

"Burt, I'm a reporter. It's my job to report the news and, if necessary, dig a little to get to the truth. I'm certainly not going to take the credit on a major news story like this." He put his arm around the detective. "No, Burt, this one will be all you. But it's going to be one hell of a pulp story when I'm done with it. Maybe I'll finally get a sale in a top magazine."

"You write pulp yarns?" Wheeler asked. "I've never read any of them."

"Well, that's because I've not gotten them published under my own name. I'm a reporter. As soon as folks see my name in a pulp magazine, they'll start questioning my truthfulness in the press. I can't have that. Neither can my editor. Which magazines do you read?"

"*Argosy*, *Adventure*, *All Western*, *Dime Detective* mostly. Shadow's good, too. And Doc Savage. He's always good."

"Well, then, you haven't read any of mine."

"Why? Where've you been published?"

Gordon screwed up his face. "So far, only *Spicy Detective*."

Burt let out a burst of laughter. "You write them sex ones?"

Gordon shrugged. "It pays well. But not as well as the biggies." He sighed. "Someday I might just earn a living making things up."

"Naw, real life's too much fun. Besides, when you write for the paper, you can put away twits like Dickson and his brother."

"Ain't that the truth."

CHAPTER TWENTY-SIX

Gordon Gardner knew his editor pretty well. Sure, Gordon had hustled and broken open a legitimate front-page story. But he had done so behind Levitz's back and against editorial authority. There was going to be hell to pay.

Which was why Gordon didn't immediately go to the newsroom. Instead, he went to his house and pounded out the copy of the story.

Lucy went on to the newsroom to develop her pictures and, truth be told, soften the editor's expected fiery anger with her photos.

Gordon typed fluidly and with such rapidity that he was able to produce two versions of the story, one, a longer front-page piece, and a second, shorter one in case Levitz needed to teach his ace reporter a lesson and bump the piece to page two or beyond.

With both drafts in his leather satchel, Gordon quickly bathed, changed clothes, and hurried to the newsroom. Despite not sleeping the night before, he was feeling pretty good, the kind of good that only came when he'd exposed something that had heretofore been hidden.

Word of the raid had gotten out over the radio. Gordon made sure he had the story ready for the evening edition. He knew Levitz would want to beat the *Chronicle* and the other papers to the punch, especially with the inside dish only Gordon could provide. Taking a deep breath, he entered the newsroom with a huge grin on his face.

His fellow reporters, one by one, turned and looked at him. They all wanted to applaud but they didn't want to get on Levitz's bad side. A couple of the men patted Gordon on the shoulder and muttered praise only he could hear. He shook their hands and waved to a few, all the while walking a beeline to his editor's office.

Off in the middle, head bent in concentration, Johnny Flynn studiously avoided eye contact. There was a large part of Gordon that just wanted to waltz over to Johnny and yell "I was right!" but he refrained. There would be time for that later, especially from his window desk.

Levitz's office door was cracked open but the blinds were drawn. Gordon straightened his shoulders and walked to his fate. He stopped in the doorway and rapped on the frame.

Levitz looked up from his desk and locked eyes with Gordon. "I see the prodigal son has returned. Sit."

Gordon pushed the door all the way open and stopped suddenly. In one of Levitz's chairs sat Lucy Barnes. A mischievous grin etched her face but she kept it under wraps when she turned back to Levitz.

The editor motioned to Gordon's satchel with his chin. "That the story?"

"Yes, sir." Gordon sat and put the bag on his lap.

"Where do you think it should go?"

"Sir, we uncovered a secret counterfeit ring that no one even knew existed. I spoke to Detective Wheeler. The HPD is already making investigations into the area banks to see just how far they're infiltrated and how much money they stole. Along the way, this group killed at least three men, Peter Kingsbury, William Silber, and Victor Tompkins. There may be more. We don't know. Only time and further investigation will tell. The story's already on the radio, the other papers will have some information in their evening editions, but only the *Post-Dispatch* will have the exclusive. With my words and Lucy's pictures, you are printing gold." He paused and exhaled. "Where do I think it should go? Front page, above the fold. You'll sell hundreds of copies tonight, sir. People'll be buying these copies right off the trucks. You might even have to publish a special edition."

Levitz pursed his lips, nodded noncommittally, and sighed. "You're right, of course." He indicated the photos strewn across his desk. "I've seen her pictures. They're very good. I've got more than enough here to publish a photo essay. You know a picture is worth a thousand words. I can publish four of her pictures and none of your words."

"Sir?" Gordon began.

"Miss Barnes, thank you for these wonderful images. We'll certainly use them tonight and maybe tomorrow as well. And, as far as what we discussed, I agree. It's a good idea." He picked up a pack of Camels and lit one. "But if you'll excuse us, the ace reporter and I have some things to discuss."

Lucy stood and straightened her skirt. "Yes, sir. And thank you." She offered Gordon a quick glance then left the office, closing the door behind her.

Levitz watched her go, then leveled his gaze on Gordon. He inhaled on his cigarette and watched his reporter through the haze. "They're expecting me to yell at you, make a big scene, that kind of stuff. I know what y'all think of me. In fact, they've probably got their ears to the glass right now. But I'm not sure I'm going to do that. You know why?"

Gordon shook his head. He wanted a cigarette as well but feared moving an inch. All day long, he had braced himself for the tongue lashing he had expected. Levitz could go on a tirade with the best of them. Gordon had seen it, had been on the receiving end more than once, and could take it.

But this calm Levitz was something else entirely. This was a wild card.

"Because you did good work, Gordon. Damn good. All that stuff you said a minute ago? That's the kind of passion I like—that I *have*—for this business. That was me twenty years ago as a cub reporter. That was me until I got promoted to this desk. Now, I'm stuck. I can't go up, I can't go down. I'm just here, and I have to live vicariously through all my reporters."

He stubbed out the cigarette and lit another. "That's why I like you so much. Johnny, too. Don't roll your eyes. He's good. You're good. There are others, too, but y'all're the best." He leaned forward and jammed his forefinger on the desk. "But I can't have reporters who think they can do whatever they damn well please and not let me in on the story."

"But you would have said no."

"I *did* say no," Levitz blurted. "More than once I said no. And what did you do?"

Gordon shrugged. "I did what I thought was right

because there was something there."

Levitz pointed at Gordon. "Exactly. You have instincts. They pretty much got you in trouble this time. The only thing saving your bacon is the end story. Had this thing come to nothing, you'd be out of a job. Preston already talked to me. He wants you out no matter what. I went to bat for you and I earned you a reprieve."

Gordon smiled. "Thank you, sir."

"Don't thank me yet. Not until you hear the end." Levitz leaned back in his chair and put his feet on the desk. "This newsroom is a little like the military. I'm the captain and all the people here are my troops. If I assign a story to you, I expect you to do it. If I tell you not to, I expect you to comply."

He waved at the door. "They're expecting yelling because you disobeyed an order. If I just pat you on the back and congratulate you, what kind of message does that send to them all out there?"

Gordon remained mute because he knew the answer.

"It tells them they can do anything they damn well please. And I can't run a newsroom that way and Mr. Preston can't publish a newspaper that way."

Levitz shifted and put his feet back on the floor. He motioned to Gordon. "Let me see what you wrote."

Gordon opened his satchel and handed over both versions of the story. "The second is shorter in case you needed to discipline me by shunting the story off page one."

"Oh, it's going on page one, above the fold, just like

you said." Levitz discarded the shorter piece and flipped pages and read.

Gordon sat in uncomfortable silence.

"What about Kernow? You were so dead set on talking to him. Where is he in here?"

"Turns out, he and Dr. Dickson went to medical school together. Dr. Dickson prescribed some powerful drugs to keep Tompkins loopy, told the poor guy to go see Dr. Kernow. That's what got Tompkins on that corner on that day. Kernow's got a gambling habit. He's in hock pretty bad. In exchange for making the debt disappear, Kernow agreed to break into Victor's house and steal back the drugs."

"Why isn't he in the piece?"

Gordon grinned. "No evidence of B and E, can't tie Kernow to the crime, didn't want to rile up our ombudsman again but"—he held up a finger—"Dickson paid Kernow with counterfeit. The good doc's still in hock."

Levitz smirked and continued to read. More uncomfortable silence followed.

"This is good. Lots of details. The public will eat this up." He tossed the papers on the desk. "But you need to be an example."

The lump in Gordon's throat got bigger. The butterflies in his stomach started dancing. He was getting fired. He just knew it.

Levitz said, "Go get Johnny."

Gordon didn't move. "Go get Johnny!"

Gordon rose and opened the door. Most of the folks suddenly looked very busy and tried to act as though they weren't listening. He walked across the room. Johnny watched him the entire way. "Levitz wants to see you," Gordon muttered. He turned and went back to the editor's office. He didn't care if Johnny was behind him or not.

Johnny came in behind Gordon. "Shut the door," Levitz said. Johnny compiled and stood next to Gordon. "Johnny, Gordon's wrote a spectacular piece on the counterfeiters. His story is going to be on page one."

Opening his mouth to protest, Johnny was cut off by Levitz's hand slicing the air. "But you get Gordon's desk. And you get it because you followed orders."

It was Gordon's turn to protest. "Sir, how can you do that? Don't you remember our little talk last month?"

Gordon had seen the steely flint of Levitz's eyes before but the look he now gave could have cut through anything. "Open your mouth again and you won't even have a desk." He kept the room locked in tense silence for a few more moments. "Effective when y'all walk out that door, Johnny gets the window desk and Gordon, you get Schultz's old desk."

It took Gordon exactly one second before he put two and two together. "The society page? You want me on the society page?"

"Yes. No investigative reporting from you for two months, maybe more. You only get to write about the high-society folks."

In the corner of his eye, Gordon caught Johnny

smirking. He stifled the urge to slug the other reporter. Barely. But, Gordon realized, he had dug his own grave.

And that grave was on the front page of the *Houston Post-Dispatch*.

CHAPTER TWENTY-SEVEN

Part of the public humiliation was, of course, Gordon having to clean out his old desk and move to his new one while Johnny firmly ensconced himself at the window desk. Johnny's little cadre of fellow reporters all glad-handed him, slapping him on the shoulders, and giving Gordon the stink eye. One of them—Gordon couldn't be sure which—actually had the audacity to mutter "loser" in his direction.

Others, including Barbara Essary, Levitz's secretary, offered condolences to Gordon. He grinned as best he could and reminded them all to look at the front page of the evening edition later that day.

The society desk was off in a small alcove. Simon Schultz had been a long-time fixture, having made knowing Houston's social scene his driving passion. Few other reporters shared that passion. He had fulfilled that role for nearly thirty years, but time, alcohol, and lots of excessive living had led to a heart attack that didn't kill him, but sidelined him. He had to leave the paper. In the interim, a rotating roster of reporters had covered Schultz's beat but none lasted long. As he plopped his box of personal effects on the desk, Gordon Gardner vowed he wouldn't be the permanent successor either.

Schultz's desk—that's what everyone still called it—sat opposite another desk. It had been years since anyone sat there, so large were Schultz's needs. Effectively, Gordon now had two desks. He slumped down behind his box and looked at the newsroom. Most of his colleagues tried not to look at him.

Someone rounded a corner and sat at the opposite desk. "Hiya, Ace."

Gordon looked up over his box. "Hey, Lucy." He tried to give her a thousand-dollar grin. He only managed a ten-dollar one.

She nodded at him and ran her fingers along the perimeter of the other desk. "Tough break, huh? Being stuck way over here. It's like newsroom purgatory."

"At least we got the front page, huh?"

"You're darn right we got the front page." She folded her hands and leaned over the desk. "And you also got yourself a partner."

He frowned. "What do you mean?"

She spread her hands. "You're the society reporter, Ace, and words are only half the story on the society page. You need pictures. Maybe you need the pictures more than the words on the society page, but I don't wanna bruise your ego any more than necessary." She winked at him.

Gordon looked at her and marveled. Lucy was working on little sleep, just like him, yet she still looked fantastic. "Don't worry about my ego. It's pretty healthy. But what are you driving at?"

"I'm staying in town. Mr. Levitz offered me a job. I'm part of the main photographer group but I'm mainly assigned to the society page." She wagged her finger. "We're still partners. What do you think of that?"

Gordon's ten-dollar grin just earned dividends. "Miss

Barnes, I think that just might make this temporary demotion more than bearable. In fact"—he checked his watch—"why don't we talk about it over dinner?"

"Gordon," she said, "we're working colleagues. We can't date." She reached down to the floor for her camera case. "But I'll let you escort me back to the Clavell Club. You need to make it up to Mr. Clavell and I'd love to get some more shots. What do you say?"

Gordon Gardner stood and offered Lucy Barnes his arm. She stood, put one hand in the crook of his arm and picked up the camera case. Together, they strolled through the newsroom and towards the door. Giving in to the urge, Gordon steered them on a path that would lead him to his old window seat.

As he passed Johnny Flynn, Gordon leaned down and whispered, "Front page and I get the girl. Who's the loser now?"

Introduction to
"The Criminal Sleep"

One of the great aspects of historical research is locating original source material. When I was in graduate school at the University of North Texas, I wrote my thesis on the 14th Texas Infantry in the Civil War. Part of my research involved census research via microfilm. I found it utterly fascinating to see how folks in 1860 wrote and classified everyday life.

As interesting as microfilm research can be, it is still like looking through a window at a time long past. It doesn't beat the real thing. The 14th Texas Infantry fought in the Red River Campaign in April 1864. Back in 1994, I visited Louisiana State University, Shreveport, and was able to discover that the captain of Company A had written a journal, and they had it in their archives! To hold this small document, over a hundred years old, and realize the captain carried it with him into battle was humbling. And very exciting.

Imagine my surprise when something similar happened recently here in Houston. I am in the early stages of conducting research on the riots that hit Houston in 1917. It's a subject ripe for a novel and I aim to have one written by 2017. A first step is to read the newspapers of 1917.

Newspapers are a prime source of contemporary accounts of history. For all the historical information we know here in the 21st Century about a topic, to the people who lived in those years, those events were current events. The Houston Historical Society has a good number of old magazines and newspapers, all preserved in acid-free boxes.

Back in one of the storage rooms, there was an old box, a little dented along the edges. Imagine my surprise when I gazed upon the contents.

Inside were stacks of paper and carbons. Most of them were typewritten with numerous handwritten marks all over them. Some enterprising employee of the society had categorized them by date and title. The earliest piece was sitting on top of the stack. It was with trembling fingers that I took out and read the top sheet of paper.

It was a story written by Gordon Gardner. The date was February 18, 1939. The yellowed pages were slightly curled along the edges and some of the pencil marks had faded with age, but the type font was clearly legible.

I sat and read the tale, right there in the historical society's research room. Gardner had written a basic private eye yarn, complete with nefarious bad guys and a spit-shined hero. I was quite entertained by it. On the last page, in his own hand, Gardner had written "Submitted to Detective Fiction Weekly." Next to that, the word "Rejected" appeared. Underneath, he had written, "Submitted to Detective Book Magazine" with the word "Rejected" alongside it. Thus it continued to the bottom of the page.

An entry dated May 7, 1940, caught my eye. The story's title was "The Nazi Menace." Instead of a submission notice, however, next to this entry were the words "Confiscated by E. Donnelly, U.S. Army."

The next story on the list was "The Criminal Sleep."

On the title page of this tale, Gardner had written possible titles, most of which he had crossed out. An interesting note accompanied this story. It seems that he knew a couple of detectives from the Houston Police Department, Chet Tinsley and Sam Baker. He promised them that he'd use their names in a pulp story. Turns out, this was the one.

As before, the last page lists all the magazines to which Gardner had submitted this story. All the big-name magazines passed. A small outfit, *Sensational Detective Monthly*, accepted the story. The byline was by a pen name Gardner used to hide his true journalist identity. A few months later, however, before the issue went to press with Mr. Gardner's story, the magazine folded and all the stories therein were lost to time.

I think it a good thing to present Gordon Gardner's lost story here with *The Phantom Automobiles*. They belong together, and they belong under Mr. Gardner's name.

So, for the first time in seventy-five years, Quadrant Fiction Studio proudly presents "The Criminal Sleep" by Gordon Gardner.

CHAPTER I

At the moment the bank alarm sounded, big, burly Chet Martin was giving a leggy blonde the once over. She turned at the sound but he didn't. She caught him staring at her figure and flashed a steely glare. He offered a lopsided grin and angled his own gaze to the bank.

The bells inside the structure clanged mercilessly. Pedestrians outside put hands to ears to soften the tintinnabulation. Chet didn't bother. He focused on the door. He expected a gang of thieves to burst out at any moment. What he saw confused him.

A scrawny man, his clothes draped across his frame, emerged from the bank. In one hand, he held a canvas bag full of money. In the other was a gun. His face was sunken and hadn't seen a razor in at least a week. The hat was too large for his head. His semi-toothless grin shone dully in the sun. No smile entered his eyes. They looked distant and not a little scared.

The man laughed, a guttural thing, and shouted, "There ain't none of y'all can catch me." With that, he waved the gun in the air, uttered a "Yee haw," and galloped away.

"I'm gonna catch you," muttered Chet Martin. He pulled the brim of his fedora lower on his forehead and set off in pursuit. The leather soles of his shoes thwaped the pavement loud enough that pedestrians moved aside at the sound. The cut of his suit coat, big enough to contain his muscles when at rest, strained under the burden of continued pursuit.

Chet rounded the corner of the next block and expected to see the suspect fleeing. He saw that, but he also saw something else. The robber was running towards a car. As Chet continued the pursuit, a man exited the vehicle. He was tall, with a prominent jawline, and wore a dark blue suit with a dark hat shadowing his eyes.

The fleeing man slowed and gave the satchel to the blue-suited man. Chet closed the distance running full steam. He was close enough to see the blue-suited man's smile. He said something to the thief who immediately turned and ran away from the car.

The blue-suited man jumped back inside the car and it was moving even before the door was closed. With the peel of rubber on cement, the car varoomed down the street. Chet knew he had no chance to catch it.

But he could catch the skinny bank robber. Chet changed his angle and set off in pursuit. Despite his bulk, the big police detective was a fluid runner, the muscles in his legs effortlessly speeded him to his quarry. Up ahead, the street was alive with speeding cars, buses, and the streetcars.

Chet smiled as he continued to run. The crook was trapped.

The bank robber turned around while running and fancy if he didn't have a grin on his mug as well. "You can't catch me, flatfoot. The cars, they're all ghosts, and I can run right through them."

With no speed let-up, the criminal charged into the street. Brakes squealed and tires skidded on pavement.

The thwump of a speeding machine making contact with a human body dominated the intersection. The tinkle of glass sounded as the bank robber was hurtled over the hood, smashing an arm into the windshield; his body caromed over the top of the car, and splayed out on the pavement. The trailing car's driver had to slam on his brakes and yank the wheel to avoid further injuring the fugitive.

Chet skidded to a halt, grabbing a street sign to avoid his own fatal brush with automotive death. Within seconds, the entire intersection had ground to a halt. In the middle of various vehicles and machines stalled or smashed lay the body of the bank robber.

In his line of work, Chet had seen dead bodies. There was no doubt in his mind that the man was already dead.

But the man's head moved. More like lolled to the side, bringing his eyes in contact with Chet's. The police detective vaulted the hood of a car and ran up to the man. The recent robber looked at Chet with a blank expression. Blood began to ooze out of his nose and mouth. The dying man gurgled something and Chet leaned down to better hear the words.

"What happened to me?" The bank robber coughed, spraying blood on Chet's ear, and then his eyes fixed to the sky and saw no more.

CHAPTER II

Deep in the bowels of the Imperial City Police Department, a lone figure stood over a body. The corpse lay flat on a metal table, lamps hanging above cast day-like light into the room. The figure wore thick glasses that magnified his eyes out of proportion to his face. He looked up when Chet Martin entered the room.

"What have you got for me, Doc?" Chet called out.

The other man, whose name was Doctor Lester Gibson, looked up in frustration. "Detective Martin, I have only had the corpse for an hour. What do you expect?"

"Answers, Lester, answers." Chet came to a halt opposite Gibson. "And?"

The doctor smirked. "I can tell you this man died of severe trauma to the skull."

"Tell me something I don't know, Doc. He died right in front of me." He wagged a finger at the coroner "You're making a joke, right?"

"Not a good one obviously," Lester said. He placed the clipboard on the table and gazed over his glasses at the detective. "Perhaps I need to get out more. Care to take a fellow officer of the law out on the town, show him some things he isn't used to?"

"Sure thing. Tomorrow night, a few of us joes are gonna hear the Charles Hunt Orchestra. He plays a mean alto sax. You should join us." He tapped the table. "What do you know about our friend here?"

"Not much besides the facts you already know. According to the contents of his wallet, Mickey Judd lived at 1915 Pierce Road, apartment 2B." Lester angled his head to look at the detective over his glasses. "Or not 2B?"

"Funny. Anything else?"

"No place for Shakespearean humor in your life? More's the pity. No, not much else. He had some coins in his pockets, the tabulations from the horse race last weekend, a stubby pencil and small notebook, and a card." He indicated the debris laid out on a side table.

Chet walked over and read the card. It read: Feeling low and need a hand up? Your Guardian Angel is only a phone call away. Call Baldwin 6-2001. "What's this about?"

"No idea."

"Tested for drugs in his system?"

"I pulled a blood sample, but won't know the results for some hours now. Maybe tomorrow? Why are you so keen on the drug angle?"

Chet pulled a cigarette out of his pack and slipped it between his lips but didn't light it. "I can't think of any reason why a man would knowingly jump in front of a car, thinking it not real. He must have been hopped up on the ju-ju."

"Detective, I don't think cannabis would have caused this man to do what you said. Marijuana is a calming drug that helps the body to relax."

Chet arched an eyebrow. "You sound like you speak from experience."

Lester cleared his throat. "I find it necessary, as part of my job, to expose myself to that which the ordinary criminal does. We have thugs who smoke this stuff and extol its benefits." He shrugged. "I just want to know the symptoms of this particular drug."

"And is that what caused this man to jump in front of a car?"

Lester shook his head. "Cannabis does many things to a person but making them see hallucinations isn't one of them. If this man was drugged, it was by something more powerful than ju-ju."

CHAPTER III

Chet moseyed up to the ground floor and into the thick of the police station. Officers and detectives milled about, chatting with each other, guffawing at jokes only the men in blue could share amongst themselves. Imperial City's police department, like all departments in big cities across the country, had its share of good guys and bad eggs. The thing was, depending on the situation, you often had a hard time distinguishing the difference.

While pouring himself a cup of joe from the machine, Sam Malone sauntered up. Sam was Chet's partner and, for the life of him, Chet didn't know what kind of rationale Captain Brad Wharton used when pairing detectives. Where Chet was big, burly, with big fists, big shoulders, and big feet, Sam Malone was thin, wiry, and bespectacled. There was a crispness about Sam. He always wore pressed shirts and pants with definite creases. That put Chet ill at ease. Chet was the type of man who bought clothes off the rank. If they fit well enough, so be it; if they didn't, his bulk would stretch out the seams. It was not for nothing that some of the men in the department referred to Martin and Malone as the Laurel and Hardy of the I.C.P.D.

"Heard you had some action today," Sam said. He refilled his cup and poured too much sugar into the dark brew.

"Yeah," Chet said, looking away. "Can't figure it out. Guy robs a bank, does an exchange, and then runs into traffic down on Elm just like the cars ain't there.

It wasn't an accident. This guy really thought the cars couldn't hurt him."

Sam shrugged. "Well, case closed and all that."

Chet rounded on him. "How you figure?"

"Oh, I dunno. Maybe seeing as how the man's dead. Maybe also because it ain't our case. Maybe because there was no murder. Things like that."

Scrunching up his face, Chet said, "Since you've heard all this through the grapevine, did you hear the part about the robber handin' off the bag o' money? He had accomplices, at least two: the driver and the big galute who took the cash. Nah, there's something there. I can feel it."

Sam waited a moment. "Well, I feel as though we ought to get back on the Bancroft case. I'm still thinking his ex-wife was trying to bleed him of his cash and I'm sure she was behind it all."

"Fine," Chet said, pouring the rest of his coffee in the trash can, "you go look into that. I'm gonna see what turns up with this guy."

Sam put his hand on Chet's arm. "Chet, we're partners, remember. We got a case. We have to follow it, see where it leads."

"Sure thing," Chet growled. "I'll catch up with you in an hour or two. Gonna take a late lunch." Chet Martin shrugged off the pipsqueak's hand and marched out of the station.

He didn't happen to notice the exchange of glances between his partner and Captain Wharton who stood in the doorway to his office. The captain raised his eyebrows in a question. Sam Malone nodded once.

CHAPTER IV

A quick check of the apartment houses at 1915 Pierce Road revealed that Mickey Judd had been evicted for non-payment of rent. The landlord didn't know for sure where Judd went, but suggested a shanty town down under the elevated railroad. Chet knew the place. He had rousted more than a few grease balls from the area.

Since the Great Depression began, shanty towns like this one in Imperial City had sprung up across the country. Some had names, like Hooverville, named after the last president. Odd, Chet thought, that, since Roosevelt hadn't actually cured the Depresh, no towns bore his name. This one bore the name of the rail line roaring above it: Boardwalk.

Chet got out of his black 1936 Model 48 Ford and strolled around the area. Like most shanty towns, Boardwalk had small, dilapidated, wooden shacks that served as houses to out-of-work men, poor families, and garden variety bums. A few women, with children hanging on their legs, gave Chet a wary eye. He steered clear of them at first. He tipped his hat to them, the least he could do, to acknowledge their humanity and his own.

He found the area of Boardwalk where the poorest lived. This was the area where men hunkered down and braved the elements, not having enough spunk or wherewithal to build a shelter. Not knowing a thing about Mickey Judd, Chet started asking the men he found in this section. Most recognized the cop gait in Chet's steps and were fearful. He reassured them he wasn't there to roust them from their drunken stupors and throw them in the slammer. That had happened more than once. Even the citizens of Boardwalk had standards and the riff-raff were unwelcome.

Chet didn't have a lot of change, but passed some nickels around to whoever would talk with him. Most of the men reeked of cheap booze and general uncleanliness. Chet did his best to breathe through his mouth when he interviewed them. He kept hitting dead ends. He was beginning to wonder if they were keeping things from him until he asked Isaiah Johnson.

Isaiah Johnson, a Negro, was also a veteran of the Great War. He stank and needed a bath, but wore the only clothes he had with pride: his old uniform.

"Yeah, I know Mickey," the man said. He was missing a tooth and some of his words shushed out of his lips. "He and I were friends."

Chet kneeled next to the veteran. "What can you tell me about him?"

"Only stuff I saw. He seemed lost around here. Some folks, they come here cuz they got's nowheres else to go. Some make a home here, if you can believe that. Others just wanna get out as soon as possible. That was Mickey."

"I have his address. He used to live in an apartment but got evicted. He lose his job?"

"Yessir," Isaiah said. "Shore did. Worked at the sugar plant down yonder. Never said why, just that he did."

"Was he a user of drugs?"

"Not that I could see. A'course, you need dough to buy booze or other stuff. Mickey used his money for food. He drank his fair share, mind you. Living here'll do that to a man, make him want to escape in his mind if his body's trapped here. Why you asking about Mickey? He gone and done something bad?"

"He's gone and got himself killed," Chet said. He watched the news hit Isaiah and the emotions flowed over the other man's face. "Reason I ask about drugs is that Mickey ran into traffic and got hit."

"That don't seem like a smart thing to do."

"Agreed. But he seemed to think the cars weren't there. He called the cars 'ghosts.' He ever do anything strange like that before?"

"No, sir," Isaiah said. "He's just trying to get a helping hand like the rest of us. He even got a hand by the guardian angel."

Chet frowned. "Who is the guardian angel?"

"I don't's know all the details as I ain't ever seen him or been picked, but he's a fella who likes to help folks like me and Mickey."

"Picked? What do you mean 'picked'?"

"You see, the angel comes around here every now and then, his friends select one of us bums. They take'em to a shelter, clean'em up real good, give'em a hot meal, and try an' help'em better themselves. One feller, goes by the name of Chuck Causeway, came back to show us his new duds. Brand spanking new suit an' everything. He even shaved and didn't cut himself."

Chet thought a moment. This was clearly getting him nowhere. Some do-gooder helping out bums was not the tree up which he needed to bark.

"I can's see you don't believe me, son, but you can ask the angel's friends. They're right over there." The army veteran pointed a crooked finger.

Chet turned. Under a pillar of the elevated railroad, a gleaming sedan was parked. Two doors were open. Two men stood talking with one of the residents of Boardwalk.

Instant recognition struck Chet like lightening. One of the men was the very same man who had taken the cash from Mickey Judd.

Chapter V

"Hey!" Chet Martin stood. "You there."

The two well-dressed men turned and looked at the sound of Chet's voice. The man with the brown suit registered no reaction but the man in the blue suit did. He recognized Chet from earlier that morning.

The man in the blue suit said something to his partner who quickly got behind the wheel of the car.

"Stop!" Chet started running to intercept. "Police!"

Behind him, Isaiah Nelson, "Hey, don't I get a dime or something?"

As Chet crossed the shanty town, the man in the blue suit turned and hustled the Boardwalk bum into the waiting automobile. He had just closed the door when Chet arrived.

The detective held up his badge. "What is going on here? Why are you taking this man?" He bent to look inside the car. "Sir, are these men taking you against your will?"

A fist slammed into the side of Chet's face. Stunned, the stout detective stumbled, his legs getting tangled together, and landed on his back. Chet was defenseless to stop the vicious kick delivered to his ribs. The wind whooshed out of his lung like a punctured balloon. He coughed but he was not completely helpless. Not for nothing was Chet Martin known in the police department as a skilled fighter. His bulk often quieted a fight with crooks in short order, but he overcame more than his fair share of thugs in dark alleys.

Chet rolled once and got his knees under him. He opened his eyes and saw stars. He also saw the shoes of the man in the blue suit come near.

The detective swung out his left leg. He had hoped to knock his opponent to the ground and buy more time to recuperate. No dice. The blue-suited cretin stumbled and that was all the time Chet needed.

Chet got his feet under him and stood. He held up his fists in a traditional boxing stance that had won him a few rounds in the department's contests. His body was angled away and he jabbed quickly with his left.

The massive fist connected with the blue-suited man's jaw and sent him spinning. But his enemy also had training. He used the momentum of his spin as leverage and whipped a fist in Chet's direction.

The policeman was surprised, but blocked most of the punch's impact with a meaty forearm. He was about to assail the thug with the full force of his right hook when a gunshot rang out. Hot lead swished past Chet's face by mere inches.

Instinctively, Chet crouched to the ground. In that moment, the man in the blue suit jumped into the car. The driver, still holding the pistol, gunned the engine. In a spray of dust and gravel that pelted Chet's face and mouth, the sedan sped away. Chet remained the victor on the field of battle but with many more questions than answers.

CHAPTER VI

Detective Chet Martin stormed into the Imperial City police station with an ice bag on his face. Normally, Chet and his bulk didn't need much in the way of attention-grabbing techniques but the bright red ice bag acted like a beacon. Officers and other detectives all gathered around, peppering him with questions. Chet, never one to shy away from attention, regaled his compatriots in blue with the story of the Fight at the Boardwalk.

No sooner had he finished than Captain Wharton ambled up and joined the ring. The captain, besting Chet's six-foot height by four inches, loomed large in the station. His short brown hair was never out of place, his uniforms were always pressed, and the soft cologne beat back the body odor too many other men sported.

"Detective," the captain said in his soft baritone voice that still pierced the din, "a word." He moved away from the men in his command and stationed himself over by the coffee percolator.

Chet, like a reprimanded schoolboy, followed. He knew what was coming. But he had his own ace up his sleeve.

"You got yourself worked over," Wharton said. He knew any slight on his prowess got under Chet's skin. "What assigned case were you following up on?"

Chet removed the bag from his face and placed it on the counter. The bruise was starting to appear. "It's a new case, Captain. The one from this morning. The bank robbery and the man who got hit by the car."

"You mean the case that's closed?" Wharton's reflection in the metal of the coffee machine appeared like a mirror in a fun house.

"Well, sir, it's not entirely closed. If you remember, the robber handed the cash off to an accomplice and..."

"How would I know that?" Wharton interrupted. "There's been no report filed."

Smiling, Chet said, "I'm getting to that, but first I need to tie up a few loose ends. You see, the tough who gave me this bruise is the same one who took the cash this morning. And he wasn't alone."

The barest trace of interest entered Wharton's eyes. Chet took the silence as permission.

"I went around looking for extra information about the dead man, an average joe named Judd. I traced his whereabouts to the Boardwalk shantytown. I met a guy who knew Judd, said Judd was taken away by some guardian angel. Nelson—that's the guy I talked with—said this guardian angel takes bums, cleans them up, helps them find jobs and a nice place to live." He leaned in and lowered his voice. "What does it tell you that the goons that select the bums are the very same goons that got the stolen loot handed to them by a man who used to be a bum?"

The muscles in Wharton's clean-shaven face worked underneath his skin. It was a war within the captain, the war between disciplining a subordinate who disobeyed orders and the apparent indication that foul play was afoot.

The foul play won.

"I think it's interesting, to be sure," Wharton murmured. "And I'm going to consider it part of an ongoing investigation."

"Sir?"

The captain finally smiled a smirk that wasn't humorous. "While you were out getting your clock cleaned as a wannabe private dick, your partner was doing official police business. There was another robbery and the suspect had the same M.O. as the stiff in the morgue. Sam's interrogating him now. Go join him, see if you can piece this mess together."

Chet made sure to stifle his grin of pleasure but Wharton stopped him with another glance. "And, Chet? I don't care if you're one of the best dicks I got in this department. You step outta line again and I'll bust you back to ticket patrol so fast it'll make your head spin. Understood?"

"Yes, sir," Chet said, suitably chastened. He extricated himself from his captain and found his way to the hall with the interrogation rooms. He looked in the first and second, but they were empty. He looked in the third and saw his partner leaning over the suspect.

Chet knew the man. He burst into the room. "Bartie, what the hell is this?"

CHAPTER VII

Detective Sam Malone and the man Chet called Bartie looked up. "Good," Sam said, "the big man is here. Think you'll change your story now." Then he realized what Chet had said. "Wait, you know this guy?"

"Yeah," Chet said, "I do. His name's Bartholomew Cranston. He's a shoe shine jockey down on Eighth. Been using him for a while now. Bartie gives me the secret news on all the guys he shines. You'd be amazed at how loose their lips are with him. What's the scoop?"

"Bank robbery. Just like the one you saw this morning. Poked a gun in the teller's face, made off with the cash, although no one can find it. Your friend here claims to have no memory of any of it." He leaned in close to the thief and said, "And I don't believe a damn word of it."

Chet frowned. It was a rare day when he played the good cop. He sat across from Bart and folded his hands together.

Bartholomew Cranston was an old man in his fifties. The gray around his temples showed his age, the wrinkles showed his years working hard labor outside in the elements, but his hands shook nervously.

"I ain't done this thing, Mister Martin," Bart said. His voice, graveled by years of smoking, was laced with fear and disbelief. "I ain't never even been to no bank since '29. Don't trust'em. You know that. You know where I keep my money."

Chet did. When the Depression smacked America right in the kisser, many good folks lost all their savings. Bart was one. Ever since then, he stashed his earnings in various places around his house, never having more than two dollars on his person at all times.

"You got the gun?" Chet asked Sam.

"Yup."

"What kind?" He knew what kind of gun Bart carried on him for protection.

"Snub nosed Smith and Wessen, .32 caliber."

That was the gun. Chet sighed. "Bart, tell me the truth: did you do this?"

"He did it," Sam blurted. "We're just trying to find his accomplices."

Chet pulled out a cigarette and lit it. He offered one to Bart. The old man gratefully accepted. Leaning back in his chair, Chet said, "Okay, who put you up to it?"

Bart opened his mouth but no words escaped.

"Nothing?"

"No, sir."

"Okay, tell me this: what's the last thing you do remember?"

Thinking a moment, Bart finally said, "I remember the getting to work, shining shoes, and then being tackled by the boys in blue."

Chet blew smoke up to the ceiling. "Who were the last customers you remember?"

Bart actually stuck his tongue out of his mouth in thought. "Lessee, there was a fella by the name of Duval, he was a lawyer. A man, a doctor, by the name of Jones, there was that reporter you know about."

"Gil?"

"Yes, sir."

Chet turned to Sam. "Gil Gibney, reporter for the *Gazette*, you know the one. He gets a bunch of facts, usually wrong, from the man on the street." To Bart he said, "Go on."

Sighing, Bart said, "The last one I remember was Nick Tanner."

The two cops exchanged glances. Nick Tanner, ostensibly a man who ran a lumber company, was also a front for a gang of vipers that smuggled drugs and guns into the city.

Chet rose and snapped his fingers. "Let's go pay little Nicky a visit."

Chapter VIII

The Tanner lumber yard was situated near the railroad station just east of downtown. The main structure was a corrugated steel warehouse that contained both piles of wood and the saws to cut them. Heat shimmered off the roof in the afternoon sun.

Chet and Sam sauntered up to the front door and marched in like they owned the joint. The detectives could never pin down any charges on Nick's establishment so they had no way of knowing which employee was honest or which one was in on the crimes.

"We'd like to see Nick," Chet said, casually sweeping his coat open to reveal the badge pinned to his belt. The man behind the counter started to protest, then rose from his stool. "I'll be right back."

"We'll go with you," Sam said, and eased around the counter. He held out his hand to the man, gesturing at the door. "After you."

The man, sweaty in his coveralls, gulped. His Adam's apple bobbed up and down. The oscillating fan blew oven-hot air around the room.

He led them out into the main warehouse, across the floor, and to a small office. Saws shrieked through wood and sawdust mixed with the humidity to create a brown cloud.

When the worker opened the office door, a blast of cold air brushed their faces. The man behind the desk, dressed in dungarees and a clean work shirt, looked up angrily.

"Afternoon, Nick," Chet said, entering the room and brushing aside the man from behind the counter. "Nice air conditioning you got in here. Feels like sitting on an ice cube."

Sam entered the room and stood opposite Chet, both detectives making a wall between Nick and the door.

Nick, with a motion of his head, dismissed his worker. He then broke into a wide smile. "One of you boys doing some remodeling on your home? Need a pile of wood for the project?" His accent, thick East Texan, drawled each word longer than necessary.

"Only wood I use nowadays," Chet said, "is the baseball bats for the police baseball games. I'm real good with a bat, able to hit homers from almost any pitch."

"Maybe you ought to try out for the big leagues," Nick said. "I hear they're always looking for big strapping fellows."

"Nah," Chet said, shaking his head, "I'd have to leave Imperial City, go up north to New York or Cleveland."

"That's my point," Nick said, his smile fading. "Because then you'd stop barging into my place of business and harassing me."

Sam stepped forward and closed the door. "Oh, we're not harassing you, at least, not yet. Bartholomew Cranston, know the name?"

Nick pursed his lips in thought, probably trying to decide the angle. "Sure, I know him. He's that old geezer that shines shoes."

"When's the last time you had your shoes worked on?" Sam continued.

"As a matter of fact, just this morning, now that you mention it. I had to meet a few bankers, try to convince them to loan me money for my little outfit here. I know the Depression's probably close to being over, but I ain't feeling it here. I need a little help, from time to time."

"Well," Chet said, turning around one of the wooden chairs opposite the desk and placing his big mitts on the back of it, "you know the shiner, Bart?"

"Sure, he's a swell joe."

"Ever get him to do anything extra for you," Sam said, "like rob a bank?"

Nick sat there a moment, then a broad smile creased his face. "Gentlemen, gentlemen, I don't know what you heard but I'm an honest businessman doing honest work." He gestured outside. "I built this place from the ground up."

"Using bootlegger money," Chet growled.

"Never proven."

"We think you put Bart up to robbing the bank today," Sam said. "To help this place out."

Nick sucked air in between his teeth. "You boys ever run a business? If you had, you'd know that in order for a man to do a thing for another man, money has to be exchanged. I get a guy to do a thing for me, on the side, you know, like those men outside, coming to my house and fixing up the porch, I pay'em."

He spread his hands out wide. "If I get a guy to rob a bank—and I'm never saying that I did—I'm gonna pay that man. So, coppers, you got to ask yourself a question: if the shiner robbed a bank, where's the shiner's money?"

CHAPTER IX

Chet and Sam stood in front of a small, wooden house that had been converted into a doctor's office. The sign hanging from the porch read "Dr. Jones and Dr. Jones, Psychiatrists."

"These ain't even real doctors," Chet declared.

They had followed up on the other people Bartie remembered from that morning. Duval, the lawyer, was in court. Gil Gibney, reporter for the *Imperial City Gazette*, was on assignment. That left the doctor, a man called Jones.

"Maybe they're quacks but one of'em saw Bart this morning. C'mon." He led the way up the small walkway and entered the office. Off to the side, where a formal dining room should have been, sat a desk. Behind the desk, a young woman, blonde as the sun with eyes radiantly blue, smiled up at them. "Can I help you?"

Her silken voice made Chet forget why he was there. Sam took the pause and led. "Detectives Malone and Martin, we're here to see Dr. Jones."

"Which one?"

"The one who got his shoes shined this morning."

"That would be Dr. Sylvester Jones."

"By the way, who's the other Jones?" Sam asked.

"His sister, Calliope. I'll be right back. Can I ask what this is regarding?"

"Police business," Sam said.

She took the hint and sashayed out of the room.

"Who in their right mind would name a girl 'Calliope'?" Chet murmured.

"Probably the same people who named a boy 'Sylvester'."

The office was tastefully decorated. Wood paneled wainscoting along the walls gave way to off-white walls on which hung paintings depicting various Americana scenes. A soft scent of pine indicated a recent cleaning.

"Can we help you?" two voices, a man's and a woman's, said nearly in unison.

The detectives turned and spied a man and a woman. They stood in the archway to the back of the house. He was coatless, his sleeves rolled up to the elbows. His blue tie matched his blue trousers. He had a together look that Chet recognized in high-society folks.

If Sylvester Jones displayed a suaveness that could open club doors, his sister, Calliope positively oozed with it. She wore a tasteful brown dress, tailored and cut to hug her sweeping curves. The hem and neckline were both low enough to be demure but just high enough to help men's imaginations. Her auburn hair, swept back, framed her flawless face. Chet found himself mesmerized by her red lips as she spoke.

Sam glanced at his partner then said, "We're here to ask him a question. About getting his shoes shined."

The siblings exchanged a glance. He arched an eyebrow. She smiled and turned. "Why don't you follow my brother to his office," she said to Sam, "and I'll speak with you in mine. Detective?"

Chet found his voice. "Martin. Chet Martin." He followed Calliope to her office, leaving Sam behind.

The office definitely had a woman's touch. Fresh flowers fragranted the room. The walls were painted a tasteful pastel green. The armchair next to the reclining couch was stitched with a floral pattern.

"Cigarette?" Calliope offered Chet an open box. She took one and so did he. She lit hers with a leaded glass lighter and held the flame for him. As he lit his, he inhaled not only his first lungful of smoke but also her alluring perfume. He felt a little dizzy. "Do you have any questions for me?"

"Not unless you get your shoes shined down on Eighth." He chuckled dryly on his own joke. She didn't. "Actually, we're looking into a bank robbery."

"A bank robbery? Why would you come here?"

"We got a suspect who did the deed but claims he doesn't remember doing it."

"How does that get you in my office?"

"He's a shoe shine man and the only thing he remembers is the last few customers. Your brother was one of 'em and we're asking around." A thought occurred to him. "This is the second time today a man has robbed a bank without remembering anything. The first man's dead. Got hit when he tried to cross the street."

"How dreadful. Fleeing?"

"Yup. But I have a question for you. You're a head

shrinker, how do you suppose a man gets to believing the cars he sees ain't real?"

She let some smoke waft through her nostrils. "I'm afraid I don't understand what you mean."

Watching the smoke curl around her hair distracted Chet. So did her lips as she inhaled on the cigarette. "Um, yeah, right, so, what I mean to say, is there a drug of some sort that'd make a guy think something ain't real?"

"Depends on the drug. Opium is a powerful hallucinogen. Users claim to see things that aren't there all the time."

Chet shook his head. "Nah, that won't do. The guy don't use any drug other'n hooch."

"Maybe the suspect consumed drugs without him knowing it," she offered.

"Maybe, but that still don't explain how he'd go from shining shoes to robbing a bank."

Calliope sat on the edge of her desk and crossed her legs. Chet was swept up with the swell of them as well as her ample cleavage.

"Detective, there might be another option."

"Yeah? What's that?"

"Hypnotism."

"Hypnotism?" Chet scoffed, stifling a laugh. "I think the subjects would know if you're trying to hypnotize them."

She nodded. "They do, when they come here. It's one

of the services we provide. You'd be amazed at how the brain works. Some things, usually painful things, are hidden so deep that the conscious mind buries them. Only through hypnosis is the conscious mind relaxed enough to explore the subconscious."

Chet gave her a skeptical look although he still remained focused on her lips. "Doctor, that sounds like a bunch of hooey. I've seen fortune tellers at the traveling circuses do the same thing and charge the dopes a full quarter. I bet you charge a bit more than that, huh?"

Steel flecked her eyes at that moment, a fact Chet didn't notice. He still fixated on her lips. It was almost as if he was in a long tunnel and the only light, at the end of the tunnel, were her lips. She continued talking but Chet didn't hear. Rather, he heard but he didn't hear. He found himself so engrossed, he didn't realize he had been staring at Calliope's mouth so intently until the cigarette burned down to a nub and scorched his fingers.

"Ouch," Chet said, flinging the burning thing away. It landed on the wooden floor and Chet stamped it out with his shoe. "That's odd. I don't usually smoke'em all the way."

Calliope smiled. "That's okay, Detective. I take that as a compliment. You must have been so transfixed by my recounting of the positive benefits of hypnotism that you forgot you were smoking."

Chet frowned, thinking, then said, "Yeah, I guess so." There was that odor still. "That smell in here, what is it?"

"Lavender," she replied, stubbing out her own cigarette. "Calms down my clients. Like it?"

"Yeah, it just smells," he searched for the word, "interesting."

"Is there anything else I can do for you?"

"Nah, I think we're good," Chet said. He moved over to shake her hand and got another whiff of her perfume. It was intoxicating. He shook her hand and then walked out of the office.

Sam Malone and Sylvester Jones were standing in the lobby chatting. The two detectives exchanged glances and nodded at each other.

"Well, thank y'all for y'all's time," Sam said. He opened the outer door and put on his hat. The detectives exited the office and got into their car.

The two Doctor Joneses stood in their office and watched as the car sped away.

"I convinced the small detective I had nothing to do with the robbery today," Sylvester Jones said. "And you?"

Calliope Jones only smiled. "I guided him in that same direction. Just made mine more urgent."

"Then we've had enough of Imperial City?"

"I think we have."

Chapter X

"Where ya going?" Sam Malone asked Chet. The big man was behind the wheel and he steered the machine away from the direction of police headquarters.

"Wells Fargo Bank, down on Twelfth."

"Why?"

"I dunno. I have a hunch about something. I wanna follow up on it."

"Sure."

They drove in silence for the five minutes it took to arrive at the branch bank. The building was a low, two-story structure with tan bricks and rust-colored accents. Keeping with the western theme of the name, the sign had a stagecoach on it with a team of horses.

The two detectives exited their car and walked up to the front door. "How do you want to handle this?" Sam asked.

"Same as I always do," Chet replied. He reached into his coat and withdrew his pistol. "With force."

He opened the door and charged inside. Sam Malone stood flummoxed on the sidewalk, flatfooted with disbelief. Did his partner just go into the bank with a drawn gun?

A police siren sounded from somewhere close.

Sam rushed inside the bank. Chet stood in the middle of the lobby, gun brandished high in the air. He was shouting orders to everyone around him.

Sam considered his options. One was to try and talk to Chet, figure out why he was doing this. A second option was to see if his excellent marksmanship was good enough to shoot the gun out of Chet's hand. He discarded that idea almost as soon as he thought it. Too many people around. Someone might get hurt.

That left only one option: physical force.

Sam marveled at the size of his partner. Having the hulking presence of Chet Martin on your side was a great intimidator to all the crooks they encountered. But actually having to go up against the big man? This was not going to end well.

He started running at Chet. Sam's sole focus was on Chet's gun hand. Get the gun out of Chet's hand so he didn't start shooting. From somewhere in the back of Sam's mind, he heard more sirens. The silent alarm must have already been tripped.

The closer Sam got to Chet, the larger his partner became. Sam was no athlete. He was in good shape, but he preferred the pastoral sport of golf to the physically demanding football or baseball. Now he was like a football kicker trying to tackle one of the linemen for the Chicago Bears.

Sam leapt and flew through the air. He timed the jump just right and slammed into Chet's gun hand. The force sent both men spinning away from each other. Sam landed hard on the marble floor and slid over its polished surface. Chet spun around, lost his balance, and fell to his knees. The gun skittered across the floor and slid under the desk of a frightened bank employee.

"The hell you think you're doing?" Chet roared.

At that very moment, Sam wondered the same thing. But then he saw the frightened bank customers and knew he had to get them out of harm's way. He rose and put up his fists. "Everyone outta here!"

No one moved.

"C'mon, people, move it!"

They started exiting the building.

Chet stood to his full height. He cracked his knuckles and made fists. The beefy mitts looked like barbells.

Sam gulped. He had seen those fists in action. Now, the action was coming to him. No time like the present.

With fists still raised, Sam dashed toward Chet. He knew his partner always started with two left jabs and then a swinging right. Sam feinted and Chet's first jab caught air, throwing the big man off balance. Sam slammed his fists, one after the other, in quick succession into Chet's bread basket. He was rewarded with the whoosh of air escaping the big man's lung.

Sam ducked the hard swinging right fist he knew was coming and scooted away a few feet. He stood again, his heart pounding. Adrenaline coursed through his veins like white-water rapids.

Since all of his swings hadn't connected, Chet grew only angrier. Fire lanced through his eyes and Sam was downright scared. He was an Imperial City police detective, ten years on the job, and he was scared like a green recruit. Why was Chet doing this?

Sam had no idea.

Chet rushed Sam. He closed the distance fast, too fast for Sam to react in any other way other than desperation. Sam dove to the floor, rolled under a table, and scrambled to his feet.

Chet was already there. He gripped the table and shoved. The wooden structure caught Sam in the chest, sending him flailing. His arms pinwheeled but to no avail. Sam landed hard on the floor. Chet pulled the table back toward him then shoved it aside, leaving the area between them uncluttered.

Sam lay on the ground, panting. There was something digging into his side. What was it?

His gun. Still in its holster.

Something crossed his mind. There was one way to end this.

From deep within his mind, a command, a suggestion, spoke. It told him to take his gun and shoot.

Sam looked up at Chet. The big man's frame filled his vision. There was no way to get out of a beating.

He reached for his gun.

The sound of footsteps, lots of them, filled the lobby. Chet and Sam both looked for the source.

Cops, about six of them, were charging toward the dueling detectives. The sight so astounded Sam and Chet that they remained frozen in place for a moment. The next instant, the wave of cops crashed over Sam and Chet, subduing them, and forcing them to the ground.

CHAPTER XI

"Y'all were hypnotized," Lester Gibson, the county coroner, said.

Chat sat in Interrogation Room #1. He held an ice pack to his head and sipped whiskey from a paper coffee cup. Sam was next to him, his arm in a sling. His insides were warmed by whiskey as well.

"How'd you know?" Chet asked.

"The shoe shine guy," Gibson said. "There was a little prick on his hand that started bleeding. I asked him what happened. Said one of his clients accidentally stuck him with a pen knife."

"Um, how do you 'accidentally' stick someone with a pen knife?" Sam asked.

Gibson shrugged. "Cranston said the customer was supposedly cleaning his nails. Knife slipped."

"What's the big deal with a knife prick?" Sam asked.

"I think it's the means by which Bartholomew Cranston was drugged and then hypnotized. How else can you explain someone hypnotizing the shoe shiner on the corner of a busy street in downtown Imperial City?"

"Sounds fishy to me," Chet grumbled. He downed the last of the whiskey and poured another finger full in the paper cup from the slim flask on the table.

"Me, too. Especially when we started getting numerous reports of bank robberies."

"There's been more?" Sam said. He also poured more liquid encouragement into his cup.

"Yup. About a half dozen. Plus the two of y'all. I happened to be on the ground floor when the calls started coming in. That's when I saw Cranston and started asking the questions. Most of the cop muscle left to go chase down the robbers. That meant I had a little time to reflect."

Gibson stood fully erect and pushed his glasses to the top of his head. His eyes squinted with the new light.

"The robberies had to be organized. All of them. A gang could do it, of course. Plenty to choose from in this town. But Cranston and the dead guy both exhibited symptoms of amnesia." He waved a finger between the two detectives. "Y'all, too? You remember anything about y'all's fight?"

Chet and Sam looked at each other and shook their heads.

"Naturally. That's a result of the hypnosis y'all were put under. The hypnotizer has the option of implanting a memory into your brains or to remove the memory of any action. That's what happened to y'all and Cranston. Mickey Judd, the dead man who thought the cars were ghosts, had a different suggestion implanted." Gibson paused and rubbed the bridge of his nose. "Word on the street is that there's another corpse, same M. O. as Judd. Y'all got lucky."

The two detectives sipped their whiskey.

Chet said, "The goons, the ones Judd gave the money to. We identified them?"

"Virgil Pollard's crew."

"Pollard?" Sam exploded. "When'd they get all organized enough to pull something like this?"

"They didn't," Gibson said. "They had help."

"Who?"

"I think you already know that answer."

CHAPTER XII

The setting sun shone yellow light on the front of the offices of Sylvester and Calliope Jones. The interior was dark. A slight breeze rustled the small trees in the front yard.

"What do you think?" Chet said.

"They know their goose is cooked and scrammed," Sam replied.

Lester Gibson, who had insisted on accompanying them, said, "Perhaps they reckoned someone would figure out their game."

Chet said, "C'mon. Let's have a look."

They walked up to the door and knocked. As expected, they heard no sound. Chet tried the knob. The door opened.

"Think the secretary's in on it?" Sam asked.

"We'll see." He raised his voice. "I.C.P.D. Anyone here?"

No answer.

Together they moved through the house. First they inspected Calliope's office.

"What's that smell?" Sam asked.

"The same smell as before," Chet said.

"Perhaps Calliope Jones uses an air-based chemical to get into the minds of her subjects," Lester suggested.

"Including you."

Chet replied, "Should be harmless without one of them yammering in our ears."

On the top of the pristine desk sat an envelope. The words written on it were "Detective Chet Martin."

Chet picked it up and used his pocketknife to slit open the top. A single piece of paper was inside. He unfolded it and read:

"Detective Martin, If you are reading this, then you are not dead. Can't say I didn't try. Only a fool thinks he can outwit someone like me. I played you so easily."

Chet's blood boiled. He stifled his embarrassment and showed the note to the others.

"Quite a cheeky one," Lester commented.

"And a knock-out," Sam commented. "Next time, I interview the girl."

"And have you pull a gun on me in a bank?" Chet said. "I don't think so."

A quick search revealed no clues as to the whereabouts of the sinister doctors. The office was cleaned out. They traversed the rest of the house and found themselves in Sylvester's office. Like with Calliope, there was an envelope on the desk. This one had Sam's name. He smirked and walked behind the desk. Lester followed close behind. Chet kept looking around the room.

Sam wasn't as delicate as Chet. He ripped the envelope and pulled out the sheet. He read it.

His face went slack. The skin around his eyes hardened. He reached in his suit and pulled out his gun.

"Chet, duck!" Lester yelled. He slammed into Sam's side just as the detective pulled the trigger. Both fell together, Lester landing on top of Sam.

The bullet shattered a framed photograph across the room. The trajectory of the flying chunk of lead missed Chet by mere inches.

Sam continued to pull the trigger until he clicked on empty. The bullets slammed harmlessly into the large wooden desk.

"What the hell was that?" Chet said. He stood, looked for his partner.

"The last gasp of those sinister doctors," Lester declared. His glasses had fallen to the floor. He still lay across Sam's body. He knew full well had the detective had the use of both arms, his desperate gamble would not have paid off.

Sam looked up at Lester and Chet. "Why am I on the floor?" He realized he held his service revolver. The blood left his face. "What happened to me?"

Lester rolled off Sam and retrieved his glasses. Chet came around the desk and helped the grunting Sam to his feet. Chet also made sure to pocket Sam's gun. They sat Sam down into the plush leather chair behind the desk.

"Effectively," Lester said, "you were still hypnotized. I suspected that you both left here hypnotized but only Chet's trigger went off."

"Trigger?" Sam asked. The full pain of his injured arm weakened his voice.

"Yes, a trigger. Something the doctor implanted in

your subconscious to make you do something. For Chet, it must have been immediate since y'all drove straight to the bank after leaving here. You, on the other hand,"— Lester reached over and grabbed the letter on the desk— "you were the backup plan." He read the note then passed it to Chet.

The letter had a symbol on it: a skull and crossbones, like on a pirate ship in the movies. It was stamped with red ink. No words accompanied the image.

"Are you telling me that Sylvester Jones hypnotized me," Sam said, "knowing that we'd eventually come back here and that once I saw this picture, I'd start shooting?"

Lester nodded. "Only if Chet didn't shoot you both while he was under hypnosis at the bank. I think you were the back-up plan."

"How do we know that's all there is?" Chet asked.

"We don't, but likely, y'all're fine. One trigger per person. It would seem dicey to add any more than that."

Sam looked at both men. "Fellas, I'm sorry about that."

"That's okay, partner." Chet clapped him on the shoulders, a gesture that meant well, but the jostling sent more pain through Sam's body. Chet quickly stopped.

"How'd you figure all this out?" Sam asked Lester.

Lester took a handkerchief out of his pocket and cleaned his glasses. "I am a coroner. It's my job to know how people perish. Most of the time, it's run-of-the-mill murder. Every now and then, it's something like this. I started studying cases from other cities around the country. I also started keeping notes and categorizing them. When I heard what happened today, I reviewed my notes. Hypnotism seemed the most likely source." Lester put his glasses back on. "Oh, and I read a lot of the pulps. Those authors can murder people like you wouldn't believe."

The two detectives marveled at Lester, seeing him in a new light.

"There's another interesting fact you might like to know."

"What's that?" Chet asked.

"The other city where incidents like this took place."

All pain in Sam's face evaporated as he stood. "Name it."

CHAPTER XIII

Chet Martin sat behind the wheel of his 1936 Model 48 Ford and listened to the V-8 engine roar. Affixed to the top of the car, the temporary siren screamed and the red lights flashed. He willed the vehicle to go faster.

Sam Malone sat in the passenger seat talking on the police radio. He coordinated the efforts to stop the train bound for New Orleans.

In the back seat, Lester Gibson had both arms outstretched, trying to brace himself from the maddening turns. His wide eyes clearly indicated today was the first time he had been in a car driving this fast.

When Lester had told Chet and Sam that additional unsolved bank robberies with similar circumstances took place in New Orleans, the three of them agreed that it was likely the work of the Joneses. Then again, Sam reminded them, there was also the chance that they'd flee somewhere else.

Chet was having none of it. New Orleans was familiar ground, he reasoned. It would be easier to return there, especially if the sinister doctors didn't think the detectives were wise to their scheme.

Or were dead.

One train, bound for the east, was set to disembark at 7:30 p.m. One plane was set to take off at 7:15 p.m. bound for Beaumont, Baton Rouge, and New Orleans. What they couldn't bank on was automobiles. If the

Joneses decided to drive out of town, they would escape easily.

Chet and Sam briefly considered calling in backup. The I.C.P.D. could easily delay either the train or the plane. The two detectives were having none of that. They now had a personal stake in the arrest. They both wanted to be there to cuff the doctors and see their faces as they were hauled off to jail.

The two detectives gambled that they could canvas both locations. They had already watched all passengers board the plane. Once the shining Douglas DC-3 aircraft had closed its doors and taxied to the runway, Chet and Sam had nodded once to each other and climbed back into the Ford and zoomed to the train station.

Travel time from the Imperial City Municipal Airport, just south of downtown, to Grand Central Station, in the heart of the city, normally took twenty minutes.

Chet Martin made it in nine.

A mile from the station, Sam reached over and killed the siren. "We don't want them to hear us coming, right?"

Chet grinned. "Nope."

Sam checked his service revolver and verified he had new rounds in the cylinders. He turned and gave Lester and extra pair of handcuffs and a blackjack. "Know how to use that?"

The medical examiner, more accustomed to working with criminals who didn't fight back, gulped but nodded. "Swing for the head as hard as I can."

"Yup," Sam said.

"But any part of the body'll do," Chet put in.

The Ford fishtailed along the last road leading up to the station. Harried pedestrians scrambled out of the way, yelling curses at the speeding car.

"It's drivers like this," Lester commented, "that make me wish I carried a badge. I'd make so many arrests."

Chet skidded the car to a halt just outside the main doors. Grand Central Station was a chunk of a structure. The off-white facade rose three stories above the ground in the middle before tapering off to a single story on the two ends. A low awning spanned the entire front. Tall windows in the center let out the bright light from the inside. Red bricks adorned the top of each window, giving the modern structure a rustic, more western look.

Chet, Sam, and Lester boiled out of the car and broke into a dead run. One station employee shouted for them to move their car. Chet flashed his badge and grunted "Police," never breaking stride.

The three police officers burst into the central foyer and slid to a halt. People milled about: talking to each other, reading newspapers, looking at the boards of departing trains, smoking and drinking coffee. It would be next to impossible to locate the Joneses in the throng.

Sam pointed to the clock up above the entrance. "Look. It's seven ten. We got five minutes."

Chet looked around and found a uniformed terminal employee. "Which way to the east-bound track?"

The befuddled man pointed to the correct rail.

"C'mon, Sam, let's go." Chet whirled to Lester. "Go

with this man. See if you can delay the train. Go, man, go!" He and Sam sprinted away.

The terminal worker turned, wide-eyed at Lester. "What's going on?"

"We're trying to catch a pair of murderers," Lester replied. "Now, where's the main switchboard?"

Chapter XIV

Chet and Sam bobbed and weaved through the lobby, avoiding just about every traveler they encountered. They burst out the rear entrance that led to the tracks and the trains loading passengers.

The two men paused long enough to form a plan. "You go to the front," Chet said. "I'll take the rear."

Sam grabbed Chet's sleeve. "Don't forget what Lester said. They may have some other command buried in us."

"Right." Chet set his jaw.

Sam nodded.

The two detectives raced in opposite directions.

Chet ran to the end of the platform then turned right. The eastbound train sat on the far track. Onlookers and travelers stopped and watched the two men run among them. Chet welcomed the halt because it enabled him to make a beeline to the rear passenger car of the eastern train.

Chet climbed aboard and flashed his badge. "I.C.P.D.," he muttered to the conductor who stuck out a hand to block Chet's entrance. "There are two murderers on board. We need to arrest them before you leave."

The conductor looked shocked. "Are you sure?"

"Without a doubt. Have you checked tickets yet?"

"No."

"Good. Give me your hat."

The flabbergasted conductor stood open mouthed as Chet took the conductor's hat and placed it on his head. He shoved his own fedora into the other man's hands.

"Make sure no one leaves this train. Period. My partner's starting from the front and moving backwards. I'm covering the rear. Now, you are. Understand?"

"Yes, sir," the conductor stammered.

"And don't mess up my hat."

Turning, Chet surveyed the interior of the rearmost car. It was the dining car. Only the wait staff milled about, readying for the evening meal.

Not seeing anything amiss, he traversed the length of the car, exited, and then entered the rearmost passenger car. Here, soft benches lined both sides of the car. Families, single travelers, and attendants all readied themselves for departure.

Through the far door, open to reveal the next car, Chet spotted Sam. His partner walked slowly to the rear. They made eye contact. Sam shook his head. No sign of the Joneses. That meant the fugitives were likely in this very car.

Settling the conductor's hat lower on his head, Chet moved forward. A couple of passengers asked him for help but he ignored them. Another man shouted for his attention. Chet put a finger to his lips and flashed his badge. The shouter quieted and sat, eyes wide. Other passengers had seen the exchange and grew still.

The stillness increased as more and more passengers

quieted themselves and watched the police detective canvas the railcar. The stillness didn't go unnoticed.

A man in the second booth from the front, his brown hat still atop his head, half turned. Chet stopped, narrowing his eyes, recalling what Sylvester Jones looked like. His eyes swept to the man's traveling companion. She, too, wore a hat, a Florentine with a brim that swooped low across her cheek. But the lips were not covered and Chet knew those lips, had been mesmerized by them. He had nearly killed people because of them.

They belonged to Calliope Jones.

He shot Sam a quick look and a curt nod. The other detective, still moving forward in the other car, hurried forward.

Sylvester Jones fully turned. He locked eyes with Chet. The doctor's face registered surprise. It was quickly replaced by fear, then anger.

The doctor stood and faced Chet Martin. Calliope looked to see what had captured her brother's attention. Her jaw dropped.

"Who's the fool now?" Chet said through gritted teeth.

Sylvester started to speak. Chet slammed his fist into the other man's face. The distinctive crack of nose bones breaking filled the room. The doctor yelped once and fell to the floor, unconscious.

Sam burst into the car, gun drawn. He glanced down at the bloodied face of Sylvester Jones then trained his gun on Calliope. "Don't move. Don't speak. You utter one sound, you're dead."

Calliope Jones remained mute.

"You want to do the honors?" Sam asked Chet.

The big detective stepped over the fallen doctor and turned his attention to Calliope. He pulled out his handcuffs and slapped a ring on one of her wrists. "Doctor Calliope Jones, you are under arrest for murder." With his free hand, he took his handkerchief and stuffed it in her mouth. "That's just in case you gave us two commands."

The passengers in the car, witness to the events, burst out in applause. A boy who sat a few rows back grinned from ear to ear.

Calliope Jones slumped. Tears formed then streamed down her face. She shook her head.

"I'll take that as a no," Chet said. He removed the cloth and dropped it on the seat.

"How did you figure it out?" she asked. The tears had streaked her make-up.

"We didn't," Sam said. He stood after handcuffing the still unconscious Sylvester. "He did." He pointed toward the rear of the car.

Lester Gibson and three uniformed I.C.P.D. officers walked down the aisle. Lester beamed with pride then took a small theatrical bow.

"How?" Calliope Jones asked.

Lester shrugged. "I study odd cases throughout the country. I look for patterns. I've even solved a case for the police up in Omaha. I found a pattern with y'all. But the clincher was this." He turned to the grinning boy. "May I?"

The boy nodded and gave Lester the thing he held.

Like a magician who just pulled a rabbit out of a hat, Lester revealed a pulp magazine. The latest issue of Doc Savage. On the cover, the titular hero was scaling the side of a skyscraper.

Calliope frowned, then wiped her cheek. "I don't understand."

Lester flipped the back of the magazine where the advertisements were located. Smiling, he folded back the pages to show her what he saw.

"Learn to hypnotize anyone!" proclaimed one of the ads. A hand-drawn image showed a man with his fingers outstretched to a fainting woman. Coming out of his hands were zig-zagged lines.

"You'd be surprised how much you can learn in one of these," Lester proclaimed, "especially the ads." He handed the pulp back the boy. The youngster quickly flipped to the ads and started reading.

On the floor, Sylvester Jones groaned.

Chet Martin motioned to the uniformed officers. "Okay, boys, let's get'em out of here so these good folks can be on their way." He eased out of the aisle. The four officers escorted the murderers off the passenger car.

Sam clapped Lester on the back. "Good work, Lester. We should let you out of the basement more often."

"Sure thing," Chet said. "Maybe we can talk to the captain, see if he'll let you consult on active cases when we're stumped."

Lester Gibson beamed with pride. He pushed his

glasses up higher on his nose. "That would be most welcome."

Chet Martin, Sam Malone, and Lester Gibson made their way to the rear of the car. Various passengers shook hands with the law officers. Chet and Sam were used to the public's good view of the lawmen of the I.C.P.D. but Lester wasn't. He drank it in like a thirsty man at an oasis.

Chet retrieved his hat from the conductor. The lawmen exited the train car and made their way back to the main lobby. Word had spread throughout the concourse of the police action. Other travelers, clearly recognizing the trio as cops, further congratulated the detectives.

"Detective Martin," a voice called out. "Detective Malone."

Chet and Sam both turned, recognizing the voice.

A medium-built man sliced through the throng. His brown suit was expertly tailored. His shoes caught the glare of the overhead lamps and reflected the light back. His hat, pushed to the back of his head, had a card slipped into the crown. On the card was the word "Press."

Sam Malone smiled. "Gil Gibney. Why am I not surprised you're already here."

The reporter shook hands with both detectives. "I've got a nose for news, bub. I go where the action is. It also helps to have a police scanner." He hooked a thumb at Lester Gibson. "Who let him outta the basement?"

Not used to the repartee between Sam, Chet, and Gil, Lester Gibson was momentarily speechless.

Chet Martin put a beefy arm across the shoulders of the smaller reporter. "Gil, get your pencil ready. Have we got a story for you."

ACKNOWLEDGEMENTS

In the acknowledgements to *Wading Into War*, I thanked a lot of people. That was my first published book and I needed to lay out all the milestones it took me to getting that first book out. For *The Phantom Automobiles*, it's largely going to be an encore.

As with *Wading Into War*, Anna Marie Flusche read and edited the manuscript of *The Phantom Automobiles* with a fine-pointed red pen. She called me out on a few phrases that were too modern, verified my historical accuracy in other cases, and generally tightened up the prose. As always, any issues with the novel now are all on me. Thank you again, Anna Marie, for making this a better book.

And to my wife, Vanessa. Over the years, she has put up with me and my occasional brain dumps when I try and describe this "best story ever!" and I just yammer on and on. She'll get this glazed-over look and, when I see it, I know I've gone too far into the weeds. She is the one who helps me distill my varied thoughts down to a coherent story. Much love and thanks to you, now and always.

READER RESPONSE

Thank you, dear reader, for reading *The Phantom Automobiles*. I'd love to hear what you thought of the book. Your feedback is important to me and for helping other readers find books they like. In this new age of publishing, word of mouth is just as important as it has always been in spreading the news about good books. Online reviews are a new form of word of mouth.

If you enjoyed this book, I would appreciate you leaving an honest review over at Amazon or any other review site. It really helps other readers find this book.

And if you'd like to know about upcoming titles, please sign up to my mailing list.

OTHER BOOKS BY
SCOTT DENNIS PARKER

WADING INTO WAR
A Detective Benjamin Wade Mystery

Benjamin Wade's first case!

Houston, 1940

Benjamin Wade is a laid back private investigator whose jobs are so mundane that he doesn't even carry a gun. He thought his latest job was going to be easy.

He thought wrong.

Hired by beguiling Lillian Saxton to find a missing reporter with knowledge of her brother's whereabouts in war-torn Europe, Wade follows a lead and knocks on a door. He gets two answers: bullets and a corpse.

Now Wade must unravel the truth about the reporter's death, Lillian's brother, and the whereabouts of a cache of documents that uncovers a shocking story from Nazi-controlled Europe and an even more nefarious secret here at home.

ALL CHICKENS MUST DIE
A Detective Benjamin Wade Mystery

Benjamin Wade Returns!

May 1940, the last days of the Great Depression, and

private investigator Benjamin Wade isn't exactly rolling in the dough. He doesn't even have a secretary. So he's in the unenviable position of taking any client that walks in his office.

Elmer Smith, a local farmer, has a problem: all of his chickens are scheduled for slaughter. He's desperate to save his livelihood. He got a court injunction to slow the process, but time is running out.

Instead of laughing Smith out the door, Wade suppresses his pride to take the case. It seems like a simple, straight-forward paycheck. He zeroes in on a central question: What really happened the night police chased someone through Smith's farm? Wade isn't the only one asking that question, but he could be the only one who might die for it.

ULTERIOR OBJECTIVES
A Lillian Saxton Thriller

You met her in *Wading Into War* when she hired Benjamin Wade to find a missing reporter with knowledge of her brother's whereabouts in war-torn Europe. Now, Sergeant Lillian Saxton, U.S. Army, stars in her own mission.

What if the only way you could discover who killed your brother was to lie to your commanding officer?

May 1940. Western Europe is on edge, wondering when the Nazis will strike. America is neutral, woefully unprepared for war, and President Roosevelt tries to steer the dicey waters of international diplomacy and keep the United States out of the conflict. It is in this environment when Sergeant Lillian Saxton, US Army, receives a cryptic message from an old flame who now lives in Germany: meet in Belgium and he'll not only give her the key to the Nazi codebooks but also information about the man who murdered her brother.

Lillian conducts all her missions with panache and confidence, even when bullets start to fly and enemy agents zero in to kill her. She's more uncertain of how she'll react when she sees the man who broke her heart or how she'll get out of Belgium when the Nazis launch their invasion.

About the Author

Scott Dennis Parker lives and works in his native Houston, Texas. He is the Saturday columnist at DoSomeDamage.com. He is the founder of Quadrant Fiction Studio, an independent publisher that specializes in stories that will amaze, excite, and, most importantly, entertain you.

Official author website and blog:
scottdennisparker.com

Twitter: https://twitter.com/sdparker7

Official author page on Facebook:
facebook.com/scottdennisparker

Email: scott@scottdennisparker.com

Monthly Newsletter

Sign up for the monthly Scott Dennis Parker email newsletter to receive exclusive sneak peeks at upcoming titles, behind-the-scenes of the book making process, and more.

Plus, you can get a free copy of *Wading Into War: A Detective Benjamin Wade Mystery*. Sign up at the website: scottdennisparker.com.

Westerns by S. D. Parker

You've got a lot of choices in what you read. So do I. That's why I specialize in Western stories that will amaze, excite, and, most importantly, Entertain You.

I call it Old-Fashioned Escapism for the 21st Century.

The westerns I write, under the pen name of S. D. Parker, draw their inspiration from classic novelists from Louis L'amour, Luke Short, and Bradford Scott to modern authors like James Reasoner, Robert J. Randisi, and Peter Brandvold. Classic television shows like The Wild Wild West, Maverick, and The Adventures of Brisco County, Jr. also spur the imagination.

The Box Maker
A Triple Action Western

"The Box Maker" nominated for the 2016 Western Fictioneers Peacemaker Award for Short Fiction.

Emory Duvall practices his simple carpentry trade, knows everyone in town, and stays out of trouble. But when a young gunslinger pulls iron on him and makes an unusual request, trouble lands in Duvall's lap.

Now, the carpenter must figure out how to avoid getting shot...and how many coffins he will have to make.

This exciting new Western from S. D. Parker will

have you asking a simple question: what would you do in Emory's position?

Mosaic Law
A Junction City Western

What would you do if your spouse was murdered?

Isabella Gilmour woke one morning thinking it was just another day. It wasn't. It was the day the horrifying news thundered down on her: her husband had been shot dead by Bart Conway, the scion of the biggest cattle rancher of Junction City, Texas. In her moment of anguish, she invokes Mosaic Law: an eye for an eye, a life for a life. She makes a simple request of her father: "Go get Stephen's rifle."

Her desperate father begs her to let the legal system work. Will she, or will she let justice come in the form of a bullet?

A Father's Justice
A Junction City Western

A man shouldn't outlive his son. Neither should his killer.

In a searing new western from author S. D. Parker, you will discover all a father will endure to see justice done right by his murdered son.

Luke Russell was a cowpuncher, making an honest way in the world at one of the biggest ranches outside of

Junction City. But he got himself in trouble over a girl, and he paid the ultimate price.

Now, a stranger's in town, asking after Pete Davidson, the man who put a bullet in Luke Russell's gut. This stranger is old, and folks realize it's Luke father, come to kill Davidson. The gunslinger is young and vibrant, just like Luke Russell was. The old man doesn't stand a chance.

Or does he?

The answer comes in a brand-new western written in the style of Robert Vaughn, Louis L'Amour, and Chet Cunningham.

The Killing of Lars Fulton
A Junction City Western

An ambush leaves an innocent man dead and the sheriff behind bars, branded a murderer.

In an exciting new Junction City western from author S. D. Parker, Sheriff Walt Eason finds himself accused of murder, and only Deputy Diego Lange can save him.

Rustlers have stolen heads of cattle from all the biggest ranches in Junction City, Texas, including Bartholomew Conway, the nemesis of Sheriff Eason and his deputies. But when the lawmen open fire on a suspected owlhoot, the dead man is not a thief, but one of Conway's own ranch hands.

Now, Junction City's richest citizen has all he needs to get rid of Eason...at the end of a hangman's noose.

Eason's fate falls to his junior deputy, Diego Lange, a half-breed with few friends in town. Lange has only hours to uncover the truth about Lars Fulton and the strange thing discovered in the corpse's pocket or Junction City will have a new sheriff, one who doesn't look too kindly on Diego Lange.

If you like action-packed tales in the tradition of Robert Vaughn, Paul L. Thompson, or Frank Leslie, you'll enjoy "The Killing of Lars Fulton," the first novel-length tale in the Saga of Junction City.

The Agony of Love
A Triple Action Western

What would you do if your wife cheated on you with a dandy of a gambler?

John Hardwick answered that question for himself. Now, he's about to act on it.

John Hardwick loves his wife like a Shakespeare sonnet: full, complete, and without equal. Unfortunately, John now finds himself in the crucible of infidelity. He knows the other man's name: Alton Raines, a professional gambler.

John is a good man, not prone to violence, but the images in his mind's eye—of his wife in Raines's bed—puts murder in his heart and a gun in his hand.

The Naked Con
A Triple Action Western

What do you do when you see a naked man cowering behind a rock?

You'll get the answer in an exciting new western from author S. D. Parker, inspired by the TV show Maverick, the movie Butch Cassidy and the Sundance Kid, and the novels of Robert Vaughn and James Reasoner.

It's not every day that the passengers of a stagecoach in the Old West see a naked man hiding behind a rock. But the motley group of people on a stage bound for Uvalde, Texas, stop and question Finnegan McCall, naked as the day of his birth. He says he is the new manager at the bank in town and a thief stole all his clothes.

But if Finnegan McCall is telling the truth, then who is the stranger at the bank claiming he is the new bank manager?

And why is this stranger asking the assistant manager to open the safe?

This exciting new Western from S. D. Parker will have you who is whom and what it all means.

CALVIN CARTER, RAILROAD DETECTIVE

An exciting new western hero from S. D. Parker in the tradition of The Wild Wild West, Maverick, and The Adventures of Brisco County, Jr.

The Old West teemed with dogged, badge-totting lawmen, vile, murderous desperadoes, and honest citizens who craved a simple, peaceful life.

Calvin Carter was none of those.

Combine Artemus Gordon's acting ability, James West's panache, Bret Maverick's charm, and Brisco County, Jr.'s unabashed zeal for the adventurous life and you get Calvin Carter.

A former actor who became a railroad detective after tracking down his father's killer, Calvin savors his exciting life, the mysterious cases assigned to him, and the beautiful women he encounters along the way. Together with his partner, Thomas Jackson, Calvin Carter aims to make a name for himself in the annals of the Old West…with flair.

So if you like your western heroes with a little more flamboyance and your stories a bit taller than usual, then you'll love the adventures of Calvin Carter.

The Poker Payout
A Calvin Carter Western

Calvin Carter goes undercover to expose a nefarious bribery scam. As always, he deploys a bit of theater when he confronts the owlhoot responsible for murder...with predictably disastrous results.

The Mark of the Impostor
A Calvin Carter Western

Calvin Carter disguises himself as a French nobleman to thwart an act of treason that could overturn the balance of power on the high seas. He enlists aid from Evelyn Paige, his former lover and sometimes partner. Carter and Paige have the perfect plan, but when his quarry exposes Carter's lie, it'll take all the detective's unique abilities to avoid a bullet in the gut...to say nothing of stopping the escaping traitors!